BEST FRIEND
TEMPTATION

Montgomery Ink Legacy
Book 4

CARRIE ANN RYAN

BEST FRIEND
TEMPTATION

A MONTGOMERY INK LEGACY NOVEL

By

Carrie Ann Ryan

Best Friend Temptation
A Montgomery Ink Legacy Novel
By: Carrie Ann Ryan
© 2022 Carrie Ann Ryan
eBook ISBN 978-1-63695-195-9
Paperback ISBN 978-1-63695-196-6
Cover Art by Sweet N Spicy Designs

For Alecia.
Thank you for Bradley. I mean…thank you for everything
else….Shh…don't tell him. But this book is also for him.

Praise for Carrie Ann Ryan

"Count on Carrie Ann Ryan for emotional, sexy, character driven stories that capture your heart!" – Carly Phillips, NY Times bestselling author

"Carrie Ann Ryan's romances are my newest addiction! The emotion in her books captures me from the very beginning. The hope and healing hold me close until the end. These love stories will simply sweep you away." ~ NYT Bestselling Author Deveny Perry

"Carrie Ann Ryan writes the perfect balance of sweet and heat ensuring every story feeds the soul." - Audrey Carlan, #1 New York Times Bestselling Author

"Carrie Ann Ryan never fails to draw readers in with passion, raw sensuality, and characters that pop off the page. Any book by Carrie Ann is an absolute treat." – New York Times Bestselling Author J. Kenner

"Carrie Ann Ryan knows how to pull your heartstrings and make your pulse pound! Her wonderful Redwood Pack series will draw you in and keep you reading long into the night. I can't wait to see what comes next with the new generation, the Talons. Keep them coming, Carrie Ann!" –Lara Adrian, New York Times bestselling author of CRAVE THE NIGHT

"With snarky humor, sizzling love scenes, and brilliant, imaginative worldbuilding, The Dante's Circle series reads as if Carrie Ann Ryan peeked at my personal wish list!" – NYT Bestselling Author, Larissa Ione

"Carrie Ann Ryan writes sexy shifters in a world full of passionate happily-ever-afters." – *New York Times* Bestselling Author Vivian Arend

"Carrie Ann's books are sexy with characters you can't help but love from page one. They are heat and heart blended to perfection." *New York Times* Bestselling Author Jayne Rylon

Carrie Ann Ryan's books are wickedly funny and deliciously hot, with plenty of twists to keep you guessing. They'll keep you up all night!" USA Today Bestselling Author Cari Quinn

"Once again, Carrie Ann Ryan knocks the Dante's Circle series out of the park. The queen of hot, sexy, enthralling paranormal romance, Carrie Ann is an author not to miss!" *New York Times* bestselling Author Marie Harte

BEST FRIEND TEMPTATION

The Montgomery Ink Legacy series continues with a forbidden romance between two best friends and the woman they both crave. Ford, Noah, and Greer aren't ready for what happens next.

I fell for my best friend long before I knew what that meant. Only I know he'll never love me back.

He's stuck in his head and his past demons and can't see what is right in front of him.

But when Greer loses her home and needs a place to stay, both Noah and I know the only place she belongs is with us—in every way possible.

Now I'm falling for both of my roommates and trying to keep the people I protect safe.

Only someone is coming for them, and I can't stop the inevitable fall.

I just have to hope that we made the right choices and that one day soon Noah and Greer will finally see who we can be.

Before we lose it all…or I finally walk away for good.

Chapter 1
NOAH

THERE WERE TIMES I LOVED MY JOB. THEN THERE WERE times I wondered if being a Hollywood body double showing my ass or even my dick would be easier. Though then I wondered if my ass and dick were even good enough for TV and movies. Perhaps I needed to do more squats, or ignore the fact that my job gave me such a headache that I was considering just selling myself.

There was seriously something wrong with me, and I probably needed more sleep, but I knew my dick could make good TV. Maybe I could go into porn. I mean, I did set up cameras for a living, though that wasn't the only thing that I did. But it was one thing to set up cameras for security and be a bodyguard and ensure that the security layout for businesses and high-profile clients was set up. It was a whole other thing to set up cameras and a ring light in your bedroom to try to get the perfect angle as you were thrusting.

Hmm, yes, that could work. I could do that until nobody wanted to see what I was doing anymore and hoard my money like a dragon. Anything would be easier than listening to this client on the phone complaining that the cameras she bought weren't the right color of taupe.

I didn't even know what color taupe was. But here I was—thinking about going into porn or becoming a body double so I wouldn't have to deal with color schemes.

There really was something seriously wrong with me.

"Understood, Mrs. Wiseman. We will go in and change the cameras to a gray we have on hand. That should work with your color scheme?" I asked, though in reality I didn't care. However, she was a paying client, and satisfaction was our guarantee.

Hey, that could be the tagline for my new porn career. *Satisfaction*, that was the way to go. My lips twitched and, considering nothing funny was going on over the call, my best friend Ford raised his brow at me from his desk across the room.

I shook my head, knowing I had no need to explain what I was thinking.

No, let's not even get into that.

"Okay, we've got you. You're on the calendar, and I will send out Daisy to work on that." I paused as the woman screeched on the line, and I nodded though she couldn't see me. "Understood, I'll send Kane or Kingston. We've got you. Thank you again."

I hung up and rubbed my temples as Ford glared at me from his desk.

Montgomery Security was a family-run business, though over half of our staff weren't Montgomerys at all. They were either friends, or people who were simply damn good at their jobs. We had our main staff who worked in this building and on projects, then at least twenty others who were contractors, but were still employed through us and received benefits.

Ford wasn't a Montgomery, he was a Cage, and though his family was bigger than mine in some respects, my family tended to adopt anyone in their periphery. Ford's brothers didn't want him to be adopted into my family, but Ford didn't really have a choice. Not when it came to Montgomerys. We were cult-like in that way.

"You're part of cybersecurity, and are the big boss, why the hell are you taking installation questions?" Ford asked, brow furrowed.

I shrugged, it was a good question. I was just unlucky enough to be the one answering the phone. "Well, with

Aria no longer working on this side of things, we're playing catch up. Daisy, Kane, Kingston, Gus, and Jennifer are all out. They're working because apparently we like to do a thousand things at once and we have overbooked."

"We're not overbooked. The clients are just adding things on at the last minute, and we're trying to satisfy them."

I pressed my lips together so I wouldn't laugh at the word *satisfy*, but Ford saw me. That was the problem when it came to Ford. He was my best friend, had been since we were kids. He was also my roommate, and occasional fuck buddy. No matter what I did, Ford always saw beneath the surface. Even when I did my best not to let him.

That was the problem with us. One of the many, anyway. Ford always saw too much, and I did my best to act aloof so he wouldn't.

It always failed.

Another problem was I couldn't seem to understand Ford. Somehow, in the last year or so, things had changed, and I couldn't read my best friend's face.

That had to be on me. Not him. Because Ford knew what he wanted, and he got it done. That's why he was our number-one installer and bodyguard for the company. He got shit done, while I handled everything else and usually stayed in the office ensuring that all of our firewalls were up to date, and coded my ass off.

I stayed here and tried not to be transparent, while Ford successfully closed himself off.

"The lady didn't want Daisy?"

"No, Mrs. Wiseman wanted a man, I think." I rolled my eyes as Ford narrowed his. There really wasn't a good answer to statements like that, and there was a reason that I didn't answer the phones normally. I wasn't good at it. I was a little grumpier than usual, though I had good reason.

I had messed something up with my best friend, and now I needed to fix it. I had no idea how to do that, and it seemed every time that I tried to fix it, I failed somewhere else.

"Daisy's going to be pissed when she hears about that," Ford said, speaking of one of our lead installers, and my cousin.

Technically Daisy was a second cousin, because her stepmother and my mother were cousins, but when it came to Montgomerys, we didn't care about little things like that. We were more of the mindset of once you're family, you're family. In terms of labels, it was easier, because Daisy and I were of the same generation, to say we were cousins. Daisy was also a couple of years older than me and could kick my ass. Not that I would ever let her.

Or, at least I would try not to let her.

"Daisy would be pissed, but we're not going to tell her. Got me?"

Ford just raised that brow.

I hated when he did that. He was way too sexy. And I was doing my best not to think about my best friend as sexy. We had our new routine of ignoring the fact that we'd slept together a few times, and it always ended up being angry sex. At least on my part. I had no idea what Ford was thinking, and that was our problem. One of many.

So now Ford and I were just best friends, coworkers, and roommates. It wasn't complicated at all.

Even I could hear the sarcasm in my mental voice.

"I guess she wants to watch a man with muscles lift things and change out the cameras. And honestly, I wouldn't want to force Daisy to work with this woman."

"But you'll force one of your other cousins?" Ford asked.

I shrugged. "Well, Kane and Kingston are family. I'm allowed to do things like that."

"Only not Daisy, because you're afraid of her?"

I looked around, as if she would jump from behind a corner. And, knowing Daisy, she was sneaky enough to do that. "No. And I have no idea why you keep bringing that up. Don't make her hate me. She punches really hard." I jokingly rubbed my shoulder where she had last punched me in a sign of solidarity. It hurt, because she was fucking strong and had been annoyed.

"You won't inflict this client on Gus or Jennifer?" Ford asked.

"Well, they're new, and that would be rude. Plus, Kane annoyed me last week at the hockey game, so I might put this on him."

"Good, at least we're doing our best to put all of your issues into work. Makes things easy."

I flipped him off, and Ford just beamed at me with his bright eyes and perfect smile.

I swallowed hard and did my best not to think about that. Ford really did have that perfect smile.

No, I wasn't going to go there. It just made things harder for us.

"Do you want some coffee?" Ford asked as he rubbed the back of his neck.

I couldn't read his face. And again, that was a fucking problem. I didn't know if Ford wanted to walk a couple of doors down to the coffee place just to get caffeine and some sugar, or if he wanted to see a certain person working behind the counter.

I studied his face, and because he was doing his best to look nonchalant, I could finally read him, just for an instant, before he blinked it away.

I did my best to ignore the sense of relief hitting me.

I didn't want to worry like this so much. I wanted to move on. Only, it wasn't easy.

"Coffee's good. Just thought you'd like it."

"I do. I like coffee."

Again, there was subtext. Both Ford and I had been attracted to Greer the moment we met her. She had long brown hair with honey highlights, high cheekbones, kissable lips, and big eyes that seemed to see everything, and yet never hinted at what she was thinking.

Greer was hot, and because both Ford and I were attracted to her, neither of us would make a move.

We had tried a poly relationship once, though it couldn't even really be called a relationship. It was just us having sex with a woman that we both liked, and wanted to see if she liked being with two men. But she hadn't liked the fact that Ford and I touched each other. We hadn't done more than graze fingers, or slide our hands up and down each other's backs. You couldn't help it when tangled in a bed with a woman between you.

She hadn't liked that, had wanted to be the center of attention, and while we agreed for that relationship, it ended up being too much for her, and Ford and I hadn't enjoyed it as much as we wanted to.

We weren't going to put Greer between us because we didn't want to ruin everything. Of course, now I was thinking about Greer between us, all those limbs and sweaty bodies. My cock pressed against my jeans. No, I was not going to think about that.

We weren't going to go poly, although my parents were poly, and I had grown up in a world where it was normal. My parents were the original Montgomery triad, as everyone put it, and that meant I had grown up with two dads and a mom. And all three of them loved each other, and they made it seem like that was just a normal part of life, and while it was, not everyone thought so. So I had also grown up with other families not wanting their children to hang out with me, or the fact that my first girlfriend's father had literally threatened me with a gun because I dared to mention my seemingly unusual family life. He called me all sorts of names, and then my dad, and the man who had taught me all I knew about the security business—Border—had taken care of it for me.

I never knew what was said, only that if Border was there, it was because my other dad, Jake, was holding my mother back from doing it herself. Mom would've probably ended up in jail, but everything would've ended the same way. With the man never threatening me again, but me never seeing that girl again, either.

I grew up with a family that loved me, knowing that other families might not understand my homelife. So me having a few poly moments with my best friend and another woman had just made sense—until it hadn't.

Because Ford didn't want me that way, or at least not in the way I was able to give, and I didn't want to hurt that little barista because Ford and I were messed up.

I hadn't even realized I was staring into space until Ford came up and punched my shoulder where Daisy had the day before. I frowned and rubbed the aching spot.

"Why is everyone so violent?" I grumbled.

"Because you're not paying attention. Come on, let's go get coffee."

"We can't just leave the place closed."

"You won't, we're here," Gus said as he walked in. He had dark hair, a large build, and looked like he could break you with his pinky. Which was good for us because he was usually the one that we sent in when we needed a bruiser lookalike for a bodyguard. The tiny woman beside him was his partner on most shifts. When Jennifer walked into a room, everyone thought she was weak and innocent, until she had you on the ground, arms behind your back and her knee pinning your spine. It was quite amazing to watch her work and, like Daisy, I was just as afraid of her. But I was glad they were on my team.

"You guys done with your job?" I asked.

"Yes, boss," Jennifer said with a wink.

Gus rolled his eyes. "Stop calling him boss. You know he hates it."

"Actually, I don't mind it," I said, as Ford snorted.

"You guys are a hoot, come on I want coffee. And you need it too."

"I'm fine," I growled.

"Crabby pants," Ford mumbled.

Gus pressed his lips together as if he didn't want to laugh, but Jennifer threw her head back and just let it all out. "I love when the bosses fight. It's fun."

"Just wait till Daisy is done with work. Then the fighting really gets fun."

"And Kane and Kingston. I don't know how we ended up with five bosses though," Jennifer said. She frowned looking between us. "Seriously, at least you guys know what you're doing."

"Or at least we pretend really well," I said, deadpan.

Jennifer gave me a thumbs-up as she moved out of the way of the door. "I would love a crème brûlée latte."

"What the hell is that?" I asked.

"Just the best thing ever, and it is one of the weekly specials on Greer's menu. I am so glad that they opened the coffee shop only a couple doors down. I am very spoiled."

"We're all spoiled. It's a lot better than the coffee shop that was in before Greer and Raven bought the bakery."

Gus nodded as he went to his desk. The whole office was open concept, our desks all outside of the back offices. That way we could work together on things, but there were also secure rooms where we could work on sensitive material. Considering we were a security business, we didn't need everything out in the open, but we also needed to work as a unit. Each office in the back was made for anyone, and were secure. I liked the way we made this work. It was different than the way my dad had run his business, since he had been solo. We worked as a unit, and not only installed security systems, we tested them, and were security ourselves. We tried to keep the people that we secured safe. And we didn't fail, at least, that's what I told myself. Because we had failed. I had failed. My job was not only testing the cybersecurity of each of our systems, but it was running background checks beyond what some of my team could do.

And I had missed a big one.

Because on the other side of that coffee shop had once been a bike shop. And the man that owned it had passed every single check that our family had put him through. Because the Montgomerys owned this building, and everybody working in this building had to be above reproach. But Wyatt hadn't been. No, not only did he kidnap and hurt his ex-girlfriend, but he hurt Raven. Had taken her from our cousin Sebastian, and I would never forgive myself for nearly being too late. For fucking up and letting her get hurt. Raven was family, and I had let my family down.

Ford punched me again and I frowned at him. "What?"

"Get out of your head. We're going to go get your coffee. Maybe getting some fresh air will cure whatever funk you're in."

I didn't think that was the case, but I nodded and followed him, ignoring the worried looks that both Gus and Jennifer gave me. They hadn't been working for us when Wyatt had opened his business, so they didn't realize I was the screw up. I would find a way to atone. But I still felt guilty as hell.

"Are you done pouting?"

"I don't pout."

"Sure you don't. Not at all."

I flipped off my best friend, and he just smiled at me.

"No thanks. We already tried that remember?"

I nearly tripped over my feet as we walked past the tattoo shop my family owned and headed towards the bakery café.

Ford never joked about us fucking. He never brought it up, because we weren't ever going to do it again. What the hell was going on with him?

Maybe I did need coffee.

"Are they almost done with the new part of the building?" I asked, pointing towards the end of the area where Wyatt's bike shop had been.

We had left it empty for a bit, not knowing what to

do. Not only had the authorities needed to comb over everything for evidence and to see if Wyatt had done anything else, it had felt weird to put anything else in there.

"They're adding the extension and splitting up the place. The space was really too big for the bike shop anyway." Ford paused. "Let's not talk about him anymore."

"Damn fine with me," I growled.

"The office and gallery should be ready to be set up soon. It's a whole lot of construction, and I'm glad that Raven and Greer don't mind the noise."

"I'm just sorry they're dealing with it," I said as we walked inside.

The place smelled of baked goods and coffee, and my stomach growled. I hadn't even realized I was hungry until I walked inside.

Greer stood there, a sad smile on her face as she waved at us, and we made our way to the front counter.

"Hey there," Ford said.

"Hey. I didn't think you guys were coming in today. It's a bit late for you."

I shrugged and stuffed my hands in my pockets. It was always so weird to talk to Greer. I didn't know what was wrong with me. I wasn't usually like this, but I was off my game. Ford, however, didn't seem to be.

"We had a busy workday, and Daisy brought us coffee from your place earlier."

"Oh, that must have been from Raven. I came in late today."

There was something about the way she said it that made me frown.

"What's wrong, Greer?" I asked, my voice low. She looked around the busy area, as if afraid to be over-heard, but there was no one else behind us. People were settled at their chairs and tables with big coffee cups and their meals, but nobody was waiting other than us.

Greer just shrugged. "Matt and I broke up this morning. It took me a little while to get ready for the day and come in. Thankfully, Raven had it handled. But yeah."

I froze, not knowing what to say. Greer and Matt had been dating for a few months, and I hadn't really liked the guy. I knew that was probably because I was attracted to Greer and didn't think anyone was good enough for her.

From the sadness dripping off her, I wanted to find Matt and punch him. Or run another background check. And yes, I had done that. Sue me. It hadn't been a full one, nothing illegal. But I'd wanted to make sure she was safe.

And Greer would never know I had done that. Only Ford knew, and he hadn't stopped me.

While I was thinking though, Ford immediately went around the counter and brought Greer close into a tight hug.

"I'm sorry." He kissed the top of her head, and I ignored the little clutch of jealousy. Because it really wasn't jealousy, it was something that said "that is right."

"I'm fine." Greer shrugged in Ford's arms but didn't let him go. In fact, the two of them stood there behind the counter, holding each other, as I stood awkwardly on the other side with my hands in my pockets.

"What happened? Do you need us to beat him up?" I asked, the words coming out of my mouth before I even thought.

Greer laughed. "No. I'm the one that sort of ended it. I think. We had a fight over my long hours, and then Matt said that if I loved him, I'd spend more time with him. And I realized that I didn't love him and I wouldn't ever. You're supposed to know when you fall, right? Or at least know when it might happen. And now I'm at work, something he hated because I do it too often, but I'm a business owner. What did he think?"

"Asshole," I said at the exact same time as Ford. We met each other's gazes, and I ignored the heat there, because it was just a memory. It wasn't real anymore.

Ford and I were better off as friends and roommates. And the moment I realized that, Ford would be able to move on.

And from the way he still held Greer, and the way she smiled up at him, I figured that maybe Greer could be what he needed. Once she was ready.

And that meant I needed to stop watching both of them. Not just Ford, but Greer too.

Things would be better when I moved on. Or at least got back to reality.

My best friend wasn't for me. Nor was the woman in his arms.

And once I understood that, I'd be better off.

I just had to ignore the temptations first.

Chapter 2
GREER

I SMELLED LIKE COFFEE, SUGAR, AND BAKED GOODS. IN other words, I smelled like my favorite things.

It had been a long day, and considering I hadn't slept the night before, I was honestly surprised I was still on my feet.

"Are you heading home?" Raven asked as she pushed her hair back from her face. She had added a few additional pink streaks recently and it made her even more adorable. I loved that Raven seemed like the sweetest, quietest of the bunch, and then ended up with funky hair, a few more piercings than me, and could stay up longer than I could and party the night away, with her boyfriend, if they weren't staying at home and watching movies with Sebastian's daughter.

"Yes. Although you should be heading home first.

You opened. I came in late." I winced as I said it, hating myself for even doing it.

I was never late. Nor was Raven. We both worked our asses off since we moved here from Portland, opening up a bakery and coffee shop that would be exactly what we needed. I was blessed when it came to Raven. She was my best friend and family, in a way that even my brothers weren't.

There were reasons that my brothers and I weren't close, and it had nothing to do with them. Nor did it truly have anything to do with me.

My family was screwed up for its own reasons, but no matter what, I knew I could rely on Raven. The fact that we had moved to Colorado, her former home, and now owned our new place, meant that I trusted her with everything.

So me being late because I was tired and heart-broken over the fact that someone I thought was a nice guy thought I was a little too much for him, hurt.

I didn't want to be a flake. Raven wasn't a flake either; my goal had always been for us to be equal partners.

Not her having to cover for me because I was tired.

"Sebastian is picking up Nora from her Girl Scouts camping trip today, and they're going to be late. They get some daddy and daughter time, and I don't want to sit at home alone. So, I'm hanging out here. You can go home if you want. You don't have to close."

My heart twinged, and though both of us were still technically working in the back, I reached out and hugged my best friend.

"I'm glad you and Sebastian had alone time though. I know it sucks having Nora gone overnight, but it must be nice for the two of you."

I loved Sebastian. He was damn perfect for Raven, even though the two of them had gone through a few rough patches to get to where they were. And Nora was the most adorable five-year-old ever. They just clicked, the three of them. I knew that they were going to make an amazing family when they were ready to make it official.

Raven had already moved in, the house next door being rented out to another family. It happened quick, far quicker than I had expected, but I wasn't surprised. The two of them were meant for each other, and it just made sense.

I wished I could find that. I wasn't very good at it.

As was evidenced by Matt dumping me right when I thought we were getting it right.

"I'm glad that Sebastian and I had alone time, too. Tonight, when I get home, there will be dinner waiting for me, and my family." She smiled softly, her eyes getting that dreamy look they got every time she thought about Sebastian and Nora. I was so damn happy for Raven.

"You're making him cook?" I teased, knowing that Sebastian was a good cook, but Raven was better. And she was the absolute best baker I had ever met. Hence why I began this company with my best friend.

"Oh, he's picking up food. That was the deal, and it makes Nora happy. Seriously though, there's a couple more hours, Frank is closing anyway, and Jasmine wants a couple more hours for the week. You don't have to stay the whole evening."

"I love you. And yes, Jasmine does need a couple more hours, but that doesn't mean that I need to go home."

"I'm not kicking you out. But I am saying maybe it's okay if you take some time off."

I started on another order while Raven worked on the brioche that would take overnight to prove.

"So you're saying that I need some time to wallow?" I ask, only sounding a little sullen.

"That's not what I'm saying at all," Raven said with a sigh, mixing ingredients together with the recipe beside her even though she wasn't even looking at it. I was working on four different kinds of lattes at once, making my foam art, even though I never realized that would be part of my life. But here I was, and I enjoyed it, I enjoyed making people happy. Coffee was a way of life, and while it could be addicting, it was just a piece of home. I loved making the perfect first taste, and then the second taste even better. That was the problem with some coffee places—you had that perfect first taste, and then it got bitter. I wasn't about to do that. No, I found that balance, no matter what milk substitute or sugar substitute that they needed.

We had nearly every type of milk here, and made our own nut milk with a blender and emulsifier. We had oat milk, almond made from organic and sustainably sourced almond farms, pistachio, goat, and countless others. The only nut milk we didn't have was cashew, and that was because a good friend was allergic. And since he worked in the building, there was no way we were going to accidentally hurt him. Only a few people had even asked about it, and when I explained we had an allergy, they completely understood. I could always find a milk alternative for them.

I was suddenly thirsty, and after I handed off the finished lattes to Jasmine, I worked on a small cup of decaf for myself. I didn't need any extra coffee, and while some people thought that decaf was a way to ruin the bean, I thought that enjoying coffee without adding too much caffeine to your system was a way to go.

"Earth to Greer, you doing okay?"

I shrugged. "What? Did I miss something?"

"I just asked what exactly you and Matt fought

about, and you didn't seem to be hearing me. You were focused on your foam art, which I understand. We are working here, but you also can talk to me."

I sighed, sipped my drink, and smiled at the taste of hazelnut, oat, and the perfect crisp blend of my decaf. I needed to work on finding another bean.

Nobody complained, but I always wanted more. And maybe that was my problem.

"I'm having an annoying day."

"Because of Matt?"

"I wish you wouldn't say his name."

"I'm sorry."

"No, I'm sorry. I'm just in a shitty mood. Maybe you're right, maybe it is because of him. Maybe I just feel like I'm in a funk. He dumped me, even though I told the guys I'm the one who sort of ended it. Matt already had one foot out the door."

"Did he say why? You guys seemed to be hitting it off. And I liked that for these past couple of months you've been smiling more and dancing around and feeling settled. After all, you followed me here to Denver when I wanted to be closer to my family, and took a chance on a new venture. But Portland was your home."

I shrugged uncomfortably, going through the next order. "Portland *was* my home. And then Seattle was my home, then Portland again, then Seattle, then Portland. You know, I never stayed in Oregon long enough to actually have a full year of school once my parents divorced the first time."

Raven winced and I shrugged, grateful for the lull in orders so I could start working on paperwork.

"I love my parents, and I hate them. Portland was home. Seattle was sometimes home, but now Denver's home. I love it. I love the people." I liked being with certain people more, but I didn't say that. There were rules, and crushing on the hot guys in the office next door who happen to be your friends, and were most likely hot for each other, was not allowed.

"Well, I'm glad that you're here. Denver was my home growing up, and now will be my home for a very long time if the Montgomerys have anything to say about it."

I snorted, thinking about the complex and ever-growing Montgomery family that seemed to rule the state of Colorado. The co-owner of our franchise and coffee house, Latte on the Rocks, wasn't a Montgomery, but she was married to a coworker of the Montgomerys. And those coworkers were all parents or cousins of the Montgomerys that happened to own and work in this building. Raven was dating a Montgomery, and our friend Brooke was married to a Montgomery, and our friend Lake was an *actual* Montgomery. And one of the guys that I tried not to think about was a Montgomery. Technically, he was a Montgomery-Gallagher since his mother was the Montgomery and one of his fathers was the Gallagher, but I tried not to think about Noah.

Or Ford.

I shouldn't dwell on that, especially when I was heartbroken over the fact that Matt had dumped me.

"Matt said I wasn't focused," I said, after my thoughts had rambled so much they just proved the point for him.

"Are you kidding me? That's idiotic. You are twenty-five, you own your own business, you have a college degree, and you make the best damn coffee in the state."

"It's so sweet that you think that it's the best damn coffee when we both know that I make only decent coffee."

"You do more than decent. And if you can call me the best baker in the state and I'm not allowed to complain, you have to sit there and not complain when I call you that."

"You know, you throwing my words back in my face is not very nice."

"Not focused though?" Greer said as she smashed her fist into the dough in front of her, working on another set of rolls.

"He thought I wasn't focused on him enough. I guess he's right. Between work and my friends and just more work, I haven't had time. Plus, there's research to do in this job. And we own this business. Yes, Haley is the actual proprietor, and the Montgomerys own the building, but we do everything else." I gestured towards the paperwork in front of me. "I might have been a business major, but it still takes a lot of work."

"We work hard, and anybody who is with us needs to understand that. That's on Matt if you're not focused on him. Oh, I'm sorry, if he *thinks* you're not focused on him." She rolled her eyes as she said it. "And honestly, last month when we did the charity softball tournament, it was only two weekends, and he could have joined but decided not to."

I winced and nodded. "And that meant I spent more time with you and the Montgomerys than him."

"He was invited." Raven frowned. "Why didn't he come? I thought he played baseball in high school or something like that."

"He did. But I think the fact that it was mostly men 6'2" and taller with broad shoulders, big beards, and ink all over them that might have pushed Matt off."

Raven blinked at me, her hands still in dough. "He's intimidated by the Montgomerys?"

"Why do you sound so surprised? Most people are intimidated by the Montgomerys. And I'm not just talking about the tattoos and the piercings. They're big, they're loud, and they're amazing I know. But they're not what a lot of people imagine when they think of a huge family."

"They're exactly what I think of when I think of a huge family. Then again, I grew up knowing the Montgomerys. Matt couldn't have been jealous though, you've never been with any of them." Raven paused and looked at me. "Have you?"

I threw my hands up so quickly I accidentally tossed the pen across the floor. Raven looked down at it, and then up at me, her eyes wide.

"No, I've never been with a Montgomery. I've never been with any of them. We had literally just moved here, and I started dating Matt. I thought it stuck. It didn't. You are the one that shacked up with a Montgomery. Not me."

Raven studied my face, trying to figure out what I was hiding. I technically wasn't hiding anything. I wasn't with a Montgomery. I just happened to have sex dreams about one. And his best friend. Often. And sometimes those dreams were when I wasn't sleeping. But I was never going to act on them, which was why I had gone out with Matt.

And as my mind kept whirling in a thousand different directions, clearly I wasn't staying focused enough, Raven studied me.

"Seriously. I haven't been with one. And I'm not going to be. I'm glad that it worked out between you and Sebastian, but I don't have that kind of history, and me being with any of the ones in this building would be complicated. I want this business to succeed. I want my friendships with the family and everyone else to succeed. I can't fuck this up, so I'm going to stay single for a while, or maybe go on a thousand one-night stands because why the fuck not. But I'm not going to think about Matt anymore. He didn't want a relationship with me, and I need to get out of my own head."

Raven nodded as I spoke, but she still studied my face, as if she were trying to figure out exactly what I was thinking.

Damn woman saw way too much.

"I'm glad that you're thinking about having fun and just enjoying yourself and figuring out exactly what you want. But you don't have to hide away from everybody. I can go and kick Matt's ass if you want. Or send Sebastian. I'm sure he'd enjoy that."

I smiled as Raven finished cleaning up, drying her hands, and then I ran around the counter and threw my arms around her.

"I love you. Just saying."

Raven smiled and kissed my cheek. "I love you too. Why don't you take the evening off like you should have and go do something fun?"

"What is fun? I sit at home and I crochet, or I hang out with my cat. Maybe that's why I'm not focused."

Raven pinched my side and I laughed, shaking my head, "Hey, that's not nice."

"You are hot, amazing, young, and now single. You can have all the fun you want. And if it wasn't for the fact that Nora is coming home tonight, I would go party and paint the town red with you."

"I have no idea what paint the town means," I said with a dry laugh.

Raven blinked. "Neither do I. Okay, I'll have to Google it later. You need to get out of here, enjoy yourself. In fact, I'm going to leave with you. Let's go tell the others, because we're the bosses, and we're technically off already."

"You're insane and I love you."

"It's what I do. Seriously though, I love you. Go have fun tonight. Go out. Go drag Daisy with you."

"Daisy's working tonight, remember?" I said, speaking of another Montgomery.

"Oh damn. What about Aria?" she asked, mentioning Sebastian's twin.

"I'll plan something this weekend. Okay? Tonight I'm just going to go home. Horatio misses me."

"I love your little orange cat. Hug the baby for me."

"You know I will. Of course, Horatio doesn't actually let me hug him. He'll sit on my lap when he wants to, or sit beside me. But I don't get to hold him."

"Only you will get the meanest cat out there, who doesn't like people, but will totally cuddle with every other stranger that walks into the house."

"I don't know what I did to Horatio in a past life, but I will make that cat love me."

"It's only been a few months, he'll love you."

"Sure," I said, totally not believing her.

We made our way out front to finish what we needed to do. As predicted, Jasmine and Frank were up for closing, and were actually excited to do so.

I packed up my things and headed home to my cat who didn't love me quite yet, but tolerated me. Sometimes.

I pulled into my garage and closed the door behind me, walking into my kitchen, whistling under my breath.

I was fine, and I would be fine. Yes, I was going to spend the night crocheting an uneven sock, and snacking on whatever was in the fridge, but I'd be fine. So what if I wasn't good enough for Matt? Or if he didn't think that we were good enough for each other? I'd find a way to make this work. Or at least figure out what the hell I was doing for myself.

I wasn't alone, not really. Horatio scampered into the kitchen, orange tail high, and the tabby just glared at me.

"Hello baby." I cautiously knelt down, hand out, hoping he would come to me. He stared at me, took two steps forward, one step to the side, and then gently arched his neck, just slightly, but he didn't touch his head to me. I would have to move at least three inches in order to brush my fingers along the top of his little tabby head.

And that meant if I moved too quickly, he would run away. But if I didn't move fast enough, he would look at me as if I had forsaken him, and we'd start all over again. I didn't breathe, I oh so casually moved my fingers towards him. He didn't move away, and he didn't look at me. But his head was tilted in a way that I knew that I needed to pet my baby.

When my fingers barely touched the top of his head, he froze, his whole body stiffening. I did the same, and when he leaned into me, that lovely purr echoing in the kitchen, I let out a relieved sigh.

Of course, I shouldn't have done that. Way too much noise. Horatio scampered off, running out of the kitchen, his back feet leading the way because his back legs were so long, he galloped sideways.

I sighed, still crouched down with my crossbody purse slung between my legs on the ground.

"Well, at least we've made some progress," I called out to the cat, who just made a loud retching sound in response. I sighed. "Okay, so first clean up the vomit, feed the cat, water the cat, have the cat ignore me, and then eat some cold pizza. Sounds like a good time."

By the time I finished that routine and read a book in the bath while Horatio paced beside the tub but still wouldn't let me touch him, I was tired.

I laid down in bed, book still in hand, and smiled when Horatio padded his way to the end of the bed. He wasn't going to let me touch him, but he would let me get close. I figured it was an okay night.

We had made progress. Maybe not with myself, but with Horatio.

A LOUD BEEPING echoed in my head as I forced myself awake, and I began to cough, smoke filling my lungs.

I looked around, and realized there was smoke in the house, and everything smelled like fire. Horatio was cuddled up to my side. His body shaking, I nearly screamed.

My house is on fire. Somehow, there's a fire in my house.

I grabbed my phone and tried to grab Horatio but he ran. Panic seized me. "Baby. Come here. We need to go."

But Horatio stood by my closet door and wouldn't come to me. I pulled out my phone and tried to dial 911, but accidentally hit the most recent call instead.

It was two in the morning, and while I was trying to get Horatio out, trying to think of how to get us safely out of my house, a deep voice answered.

"Greer? What's wrong?"

I had called Ford. The last number I dialed because I had his coffee order. His voice nearly made tears

CARRIE ANN RYAN

spring to my eyes, but it was something. It was
something.

"My house is on fire. And I can't get my cat. Ford. I
need to call 911. My house is on fire."

Something snapped and the fire grew closer. I threw
myself towards Horatio, grateful when I caught his little
orange body. His claws dug into my arm, Ford shouted
directions in the phone, I coughed, and I prayed.

"Greer! Greer, are you there?"

But there was nothing.

34

Chapter 3
FORD

NOAH AND I COULD SEE THE FLAMES AND SMOKE billowing in the air as we screeched to a halt. Noah was on the phone with 911. I knew they would send the fire trucks and whoever right away.

But Greer was still inside, and we had beat the fire trucks here. And I'd be damned if I let her burn alive at the end of that line.

"Greer!" I called.

But there was no answer, just crackles.

"Are you seriously going in there?" Noah asked.

I could hear the 911 dispatcher telling us not to, but I ignored her, and I knew Noah wouldn't wait either.

"She's in there with her damn cat," I growled.

"Then we go get her."

"She better be okay," I said. My heart raced as we

went around the back, where the flames seemed to be the lightest, and I mule-kicked the back door in.

Smoke billowed around us, flames danced through the kitchen, but it was a one-story house, and not all of it seemed to be burning, yet.

I put my bandanna over my mouth, and I knew Noah had done the same, having hung up on the 911 dispatcher. We were going to get in trouble with our contact there, but I didn't fucking care. Greer had been so damn scared on the other line, and I still didn't know how she had called me. But she had, and I'd be damned if I failed her.

"Greer! Greer!"

"Where was she when she called?"

"She must have been fucking sleeping, so her bedroom?"

We had never been in Greer's rental, so we had no idea where her bedroom was, but there was a cluster of rooms on the other side, so we kept going, heads down, and trying to stay out of the smoke.

There was no fire on this side, just smoke, but the fire was moving quickly.

This was so damn stupid, and the fire engine was going to be there any moment, but I couldn't think. I needed to get her.

"Greer!"

"We're here. But I can't get Horatio. He's scared."

Greer coughed every word out, and I cursed. She would die of smoke inhalation before the flames even hit her, and fear coated my tongue.

"Stay down, we're getting you."

"You're going to get hurt!" she called out, but considering she was the one stuck in a burning house, her concern for our safety was misplaced.

"Come on," Noah growled, as we jumped over one set of flames. Heat slashed at me, but I ignored it. The sight of Greer kneeling in her pajamas on the floor, broken phone in hand, her other hand outstretched to the cat, nearly broke me.

"You're bleeding," I said.

Greer looked over her shoulder at me and coughed into her elbow. She had soot on her face, blood on her arm and down her leg. Part of the ceiling had come down somehow and I could see where she'd made a break for it, only to stop moving because her cat hadn't had the sense to leap into her arms. "It's from the cat. He's just scared. We're still new friends. Please help."

"I've got him," Noah said as he crawled past me, hands outstretched toward the orange cat with a puffed up tail and fangs bared. "What's his name?"

"Horatio," she coughed.

I raised a brow at the odd name for a cat, but held out my hands toward her, keeping low and out of the worst of the smoke. This was one of the most insane

37

things we'd ever done in our lives, but we weren't about to let Greer die while we watched safely from our truck.

"Come on, I'll get you out of here."

"Part of the ceiling fell over there," she said, gesturing towards her bathroom. "I didn't get really hurt, but I dove out of the way, scared the cat, and broke my phone." She coughed again and I knew she was in shock, but if she didn't move, I'd drag her out of here. I didn't know how much longer we had in this place with all the smoke and heat billowing around us.

I did my best to make my voice sound gentle. "Okay, let's get you out of here. You don't have any shoes on, so I'm going to carry you."

"I'm fine," she said, before she began to cough so hard, her body shook.

I cursed and grabbed her.

"Horatio," she whispered, her voice hoarse.

"Breathe into my bandanna, I'm getting you out."

"I've got the cat," Noah shouted over the roar of the flames.

I looked behind me to see Noah had taken off his outer flannel and wrapped it around Horatio. The cat seemed to be nuzzling Noah, rubbing his head up and down Noah's beard.

I looked down at Greer for a moment, at the absolute shock on her face, but I did my best to ignore it. "That's Noah, he has a way with animals." I knew humor wasn't the best idea in this situation, but I had nothing left at this point. Both Noah and Greer—as well as the damn cat—were in danger and I needed to get them to safety.

Noah glared at me, but then we moved, doing our best to get out the way we came. Only, the flames had moved. Noah cursed. "Fuck, that way is out."

"The window? We're on the first floor."

Noah nodded, and I knew that if we set down the cat, we weren't going to get out of there. We ducked our way towards the other side of the bed and I set Greer down.

"Stay back." I shoved up the window, cursed when it only went halfway, then used my strength to break it out of the seal. Whoever had installed this hadn't given a damn, and if I hadn't been here, there was no way Greer would have been able to get out on her own. I kicked the screen out of the way, cursed again when part of the windowpane on the other side broke, shattering glass everywhere. The sound of sirens was a blessing, but we still weren't out of the woods. I kicked more glass out before I jumped out of the window first. I held out my arms and gestured towards Greer.

"Come on, I've got you."

"Ford," she said, before she shook herself, as if coming out of a shock. She was so damn strong. She'd done all of this on autopilot, I just needed her to do a bit more. She had been out cold, sleeping hard, when suddenly her house was on fire. She had tried to save her cat. Animals were like your kids but, unlike kids, they didn't fucking listen to you.

"You're doing so damn good, baby. Come on."

She gripped my hand and I lifted her up, out of the way of the glass. Her legs were bare, only wearing sleep shorts, but thankfully she didn't cut herself. I shook my head and held her close as Noah handed over the cat.

"Be careful, but he doesn't bite."

"He seems to love you," I grumbled. I took the cat, and it cuddled with me, rubbing its head along my beard.

Greer looked between us, hurt crossing her expression, but maybe I was just imagining things. After all, I was coughing a lot now too.

I backed up as Noah jumped out the window, and then we made our way to the street.

Flames began to dance in the bedroom window as Greer sank into Noah's hold. I was still holding Horatio, but I leaned against her, trying to keep her warm.

Greer's voice came out as a rasp as she whispered beside me. "My house. All my things."

"You're alive," Noah growled out. "Come on, you're barefoot. The ambulance is here, let's make sure that your lungs are clear."

Noah's tone seemed to push her out of any shock she

might slip into again and was the only reason I didn't scowl at him for the way he spoke to her. "Oh my God, we could have died. How did you…how did you get here?"

I started to answer, but she wavered a bit, and I cursed. "Over here!" I called out to the paramedics and firefighters.

We could have questions and answers later, and we'd have to deal with the fact that we had just run into a burning building to save our friend, but we would.

Greer was alive and so was her cat—the cat currently making biscuits on my chest.

I shook my head and was grateful when the firefighters had a smaller mask of oxygen for the cat. Horatio leaned into me as he breathed, but the cat looked none the worse for wear. If anything, Greer had been hurt worse with her coughing, a cut on her arm from the cat, and from when part of the ceiling had caved in.

The paramedics were taking care of her now, and I just sat there, cat on my lap as Noah held her close and I finally let myself breathe.

Greer had almost died tonight.

And it was going to take a hell of a long time for me to calm down from that realization. Or the fact that, even accidentally, she had called *us* to help.

• • •

BY THE TIME both Greer and Horatio were settled and checked out by the paramedics, we were all exhausted, with Horatio now thankfully in a cat carrier with a neighbor.

Greer hadn't wanted to leave the cat behind, but we couldn't bring him to the emergency room. That meant Horatio was safe with a neighbor, but Greer was stressed out. I didn't blame her. Everything happened so suddenly. We needed to make sure that she didn't need stitches on any of her cuts, and then to speak with the authorities in case there was foul play involved, all while the firefighters and the rest of the team doused the fire, saving whatever they could of Greer's home.

I didn't think it would be a total loss, but there was no way that she would be moving back in anytime soon. And, honestly, I didn't know what of her things could be salvaged. That would come soon, and we would help her deal.

But for now, I was grateful that Greer had even let us in the room with her, rather than waiting out in the parking lot or waiting room.

Noah paced in front of us, Greer sitting on the hospital bed, still wearing her pajamas, ready to be checked out. She had a bandage on her arm, and a small butterfly bandage on her forehead. But she needed no stitches, and her lungs were clear. They wanted to do a check on her in a couple of days, but she seemed mostly okay.

"Okay, I just texted my vet. I can bring Horatio in tomorrow to be checked out. His poor little lungs."

She sounded so calm and collected, but I knew that was still shock. She hadn't cried yet, hadn't broken down. She would. Hell, I would in her situation.

But she was fine for now, and that had to count for something.

"You're sure you're okay?" I asked, my voice gruff. I hadn't inhaled as much smoke as she had, but the doctors still checked both me and Noah out. Noah had grumbled about it, but with one look from Greer, he had given in.

I liked that. Mostly because he used to listen to me. Now he was too busy trying to ignore me and what the hell was going on between us—or lack thereof.

"I'm fine. And Horatio's going to be fine. And now I just need to figure out whose couch I'm going to bunk on and oh my God if I keep thinking about it I'm going to stress out so I need a to-do list. Raven's better with to-do lists, but I'm not bad."

Without thinking, I stood up and reached towards her, gripping her hand. She froze, looking down at where I touched her. Noah looked between us and gave a slight nod that I had no idea how to interpret before looking back down at his phone, typing faster than I thought possible. He was our digital guy for a reason, and I didn't know what he was working on. If it was actual work, or something to do with this situation.

"Everything's fine. You're not alone in this. The fact that you and Horatio are safe is all that matters."

"You guys saved my cat." She looked between us, causing Noah to finally stop pacing. "You got him out of the house. And he came right to you."

Noah shrugged. "We like animals."

I nodded in agreement. "And they tend to like us."

A single tear slid down her cheek. If she broke down now, she was going to lose it for a while, and there were decisions to be made. Plus, she wouldn't want to cry in public. I knew Greer that much.

"He doesn't even let me touch him."

I frowned. "What?"

"Horatio. He never lets me pet him, or hold him. When he's in the mood, he'll come to me and lean his head out so I can barely brush against him. But I have to be cautious. Like I'm petting a velociraptor in one of those *Jurassic Park* movies."

"Do they pet velociraptors in those movies?" Noah asked.

"In the later ones, I think. Or maybe it was just one. I don't actually remember. Anyway though..." She trailed off.

I cleared my throat. "Anyway, you said you just got

him recently right? He's just learning his new environment."

"He didn't take that long with you two."

I looked at Noah, trying to find the words. Thankfully, Noah came forward.

"He knows that you are his home. You're his person. So he is going to be cautious with you because he doesn't want to lose you. Us? He could take us or leave us. And not to mention the fact that you were in a high-stress situation. Of course the cat wanted to get out of the house. We were there, and he knew you were safe with us too, so he could be safe."

I was pretty sure Noah was making shit up, but I didn't mind. It sounded like it could be true.

Of course, Greer looked just as skeptical.

"Okay. Okay. Raven is on her way. Sebastian's with her—they dropped Nora off with his parents. I guess your aunt and uncle." She turned to Noah, who nodded.

"Yes, my aunt and uncle. *Actual* aunt and uncle."

His lips quirked into a smile, and I held back a smile of my own. I really liked that smile.

"Okay. Well, that's good. And then I'll figure out what to do. I still have to open up the coffee shop tomorrow and everything, and I don't even have clothes. I'm so glad that Noah grabbed a pair of shoes for me while you grabbed Horatio on our way out, because I don't even have anything to wear." Her voice started to get high-pitched.

"It's okay. We'll make a plan."

"Yep, I texted the family group chat, you'll have some clothes within the hour."

My lips twitched. Of course he texted the Montgomery family group chat. There were multiple versions of it. All subsets within family and friend groups within the family, and the major one that included over one hundred people. There were rules for that group chat. You weren't allowed to just ask how someone was doing in that one. It was more for sending out important details, or alerts if one of the Montgomerys were in the hospital. And oddly enough, like my family, the Montgomerys tended to be in the hospital often.

"Are you serious? You guys can't do that."

"Of course we can. You're our friend, something bad happened, and we're going to help as much as we can."

"The cops came in when you guys were being checked out, and they said that they were going to look over everything. I didn't leave anything on. I'm one of those people that takes photos of my curling iron before I leave the house to reassure myself it's not plugged in. I never leave candles burning when Horatio is around because I'm afraid he's going to catch his tail on fire and then we'd have to amputate it."

"Huh?" Noah asked, then shook his head. "You know what, I'm not even going to ask."

"One of my friends had a candle wax melt thing, and the cat got his tail in it and then it hardened and he was in a lot of pain, so they had to amputate the tip of his tail. I have horror stories in my brain about it, so now I don't like candles. It's a whole thing. So, it couldn't have been me, right? It must have been wiring or something."

"They'll figure it out. It was probably something that they can't tell right away. But with the Montgomerys and us, you'll get through this," I said softly.

"I just hate having to rely on so many people. And I'm going to really hate calling my brothers in the morning and telling them that my house burned down. A rental. I don't even own the place."

I met Noah's gaze and he frowned.

"You have brothers?" I asked, wanting to know more about Greer, even though I probably shouldn't.

She nodded. "Three. They live back in Portland. I don't really, well, it's a long story but I don't really know them as well as I would like to. I will one day though. And now I'm rambling again."

"Don't worry. We'll figure out the next steps, Raven and Sebastian are on their way, and you're not alone in this. You're out of the fire, you're safe, Horatio is safe, that's all that matters for now." I tried to sound soothing, but I knew that there was a hard road in front of her. We would figure this out, and I wouldn't let her do this alone, but all I kept hearing was the sound of her voice begging for help over the phone, the sound of fire in the background. I wouldn't be forgetting that anytime soon.

My phone rang and I frowned at the number. "Hello?"

"Hello, we need to speak with Greer Cassidy. She left this number on our voice mail."

I sighed, knowing this had to be the landlords. This wasn't going to be an easy conversation for anyone. The fact that Greer had to leave a message, as well as have the authorities call them on their own hadn't been ideal.

When she took the phone from me, she didn't say anything, nor did she ask for privacy. She just listened to whoever was on the line. Noah was typing again, probably solving world peace or something, and while I wanted to text my family, because I knew they would help at the drop of a hat, I didn't. Mostly because if the Montgomerys were handling it, the Cages didn't need to step in. That would be too many people in one room.

"I'm so sorry. Seriously. I'm sor—" Greer's voice cut off as she began to cry, then she nodded, though the person on the line couldn't see her.

I could hear shouting though, on the other line, and I wanted to reach out and take the phone from her. I didn't, I just stood there, wanting to yell at anybody who would dare yell at her, especially now.

When she hung up, she looked totally drained.

"That was the landlord. They're really angry and they said some mean things, and I think they blame me outright for what happened."

"Are you fucking kidding me?" Noah growled. "Why the hell would they do that? It wasn't your fault."

"That's not what they're saying."

"There's no evidence of that. The report will come in and then we'll figure it out, but it's not your fault." I agreed with Noah.

"I don't think they care. They are evicting me. Out of a burned-up home. And it's going on my credit, and I'm never going to be able to rent another place, that means I'm going to have to get a mortgage even though I just bought the cafe—I don't know what I'm going to do." She burst into tears, the adrenaline having finally worn off.

I cursed before I sat down next to her, wrapping my arm around her shoulders. She sank into me, gripping my shirt as she cried.

My heart broke, and I didn't know how to fix this. I looked at Noah, begging for help.

We knew the Montgomerys had a few properties, but off the top of my head I didn't think any were open.

Noah stared at me before he swallowed and nodded, as if he'd made a decision.

"You can move in with us," he blurted.

I blinked at him, as everything started to make sense. We had a spare room—a guest room we never used, and our friend needed help. Noah hadn't asked, but I nodded in agreement.

"Exactly. We have a spare room."

Greer stiffened, before she looked up, staring back and forth between us. "Are you serious? No, I can't do that."

"You need a place to stay," Noah began.

"We have one, and it's a whole bedroom with your own private bathroom." I paused. "And we own the house, you won't have to deal with a landlord. It will just be us, and we like cats."

Noah smiled, taking a few hours of exhaustion off his face. "And as you said, Horatio likes us. So we're someone he knows. You won't have to stay with any of your friends with kids, or anything like that. We'll figure it out. It doesn't have to be permanent."

"Exactly," I continued, before Greer could step in and talk us out of this.

"I can't do that. We hardly know each other."

I shrugged. "Then we'll get to know each other. We're all roommates."

"But you guys aren't…" Her voice trailed off, and Noah froze as I swallowed hard.

"We're roommates and best friends and business owners," I said, repeating Noah's words from our last fight. Noah didn't say anything and had schooled his features not to show what he was thinking.

"Exactly. We're all friends. You need the space, and frankly, it'd be nice to keep you under our roof for a while, because you scared the shit out of us," Noah said quickly.

I nodded, that adrenaline hitting again. "Pretty much. That phone call scared the shit out of us. So us knowing that you're safe, and Horatio is safe, means we'll be able to sleep at night."

This was probably a fucking mistake. Something that would probably lead to more wet dreams, but I didn't care.

She needed help, so we would help.

"I guess. I mean, okay. Okay."

I just had to hope we hadn't fucked everything up.

Chapter 4
NOAH

Two weeks.

It had taken two weeks of Greer living in the room next to mine for me to lose my mind.

Odd, since it had taken two years of living with Ford to do the same.

Perhaps it was because I'd already been over the edge.

Or perhaps I'd lost my will to fight the need.

No amount of working out to burn through the excess need, energy, and desire was going to fix this. We had a small gym at the back of the house. It was more of an office turned equipment storage area, but we made it work. We liked the light in this room, so we used this open space for our workouts to not funk-up the guest room.

When Greer moved in, the furniture was already in there for her. She had lost her bedroom set, and almost everything else. Whatever hadn't been burned had been covered in water from the firetrucks, soot, ash, and God knew what else.

In the weeks since the fire, we were able to go and salvage what we could, but other than the important documents that had been in her fire-safe box, there wasn't much.

I tried not to think that if she hadn't woken when she did, if the smoke alarms hadn't worked just right, we would have lost her. The fire had blazed, and we were damn lucky we lived close enough to get to her in time. I still couldn't quite believe she called Ford instead of 911, but she had been panicking, and just hit the next number rather than holding down the side of her phone to call the emergency line. It had worked out, but we all almost lost her.

I didn't want to think about Greer too much.

We had somehow found a system. A system which included acting really fucking awkward around each other. It hadn't helped that Ford and I acted awkward around each other anyway these days, because we were trying to ignore the fact that we wanted each other and didn't want to. Or maybe that was just me. Maybe I was the awkward one who was fucking things up.

After all, my dick wouldn't behave when it came to thinking about him. Or her.

I was stuck in my own perpetual purgatory, and I wasn't getting out. At least not anytime soon.

As I worked with free weights, trying to tire myself out before a long night of wet dreams and whatever else my brain came up with, I tried not to think about my dick pressing hard against my gym shorts.

I looked down at my crotch and glared at my erection.

There was no reason to have a hard-on right now. I was working my muscles, not my cock. I could work that later in the shower.

I rubbed my temple with my free hand, before I started arm curls, one set of ten, then another, then another.

I'd be sore later, but that was fine. I needed to work off this energy, the fact that I was living with two people I was incredibly attracted to was making it difficult to think these days.

I switched arms as a familiar orange cat walked into the gym and began to wrap itself around my legs.

I set the weight aside and leaned down, holding out my hand.

"Come on, Horatio. What's up?"

Horatio sniffed my fingers and leaned into my hand for pets. I acquiesced, scratching under his neck, then the top of his head. When he jumped into my lap, I held back a curse, not knowing what to do with the thing. I was fine with animals, I loved cats. I didn't have a cat growing up because we had a dog who had been abused before we adopted him from the shelter. He hadn't done well with other animals, but did great with kids.

So I didn't know how to take care of cats.

"Am I supposed to feed you now?" A single meow in response didn't tell me anything. "I don't think so. Your mom has you on a specific routine I think."

I had done some research on cats and knew that some cats could free feed because they moderated their own intake, and those who couldn't, the ones who just wanted to eat all day because it was there, had to have their food regulated.

This one got wet food in the morning, and dry food at night. And the only reason that I knew any of this was that I watched Greer do it. I watched her move around the house, helping her where I could. I didn't think she had fully processed what happened yet—none of us had.

She had some things in storage, because the house had been a rental, but she'd still lost so much.

I didn't know what the next steps were, but she was staying here for the time being, and I was going to have to deal with it.

And the cat currently on my lap.

"What are we doing?" I mumbled under my breath.

"Is he bothering you?" a soft voice asked, and I turned to see Greer walking towards us.

She had on pajamas—long pants and a tank top that showed some of her stomach and showcased her breasts. I swallowed, trying not to look at her nipples pressed against the thin cotton. And she wasn't wearing a bra.

I loved the look of her breasts. I thought about them often. That might make me a lecher, but it wasn't like I was going to do anything about it. I wasn't a horrible person. I wasn't going to ruin what we had by making things weird.

I was just going to stop thinking about her tits.

See? I could do it.

Her beautiful tits that could overfill my hands.

"Noah? What are you thinking about?"

Your breasts.

I didn't say that out loud, but it was a near thing. I was clearly suffering from a lack of sleep. Between two of our most difficult clients, the fire, and the fact that I could barely sleep from thinking about the other two people in this house, I wasn't firing on all cylinders.

"Sorry, I'm losing my mind. Anyway, Horatio's fine. We're just hanging out…I guess. Maybe he wants to do a little cat workout? Are there cat barbells?"

Greer rolled her eyes.

I knew I sounded like an idiot, but I couldn't be smart when I was around her. I lost all sense of anything, which was a problem because I knew she and Ford had a connection. There was just something between them, and I had to be okay with it.

They fit. And it would be better for everyone if one of them finally made a move. That way I would stop thinking about them, and I would stop fucking up everything with my best friend.

Because if he was finally in a steady relationship, especially with the woman in front of me, then I wouldn't mess up our friendship any more than I already had.

Maybe I would try to push them together. Yeah, I could do that. Push them towards one another so they could actually see what was right in front of them.

That would make things easier.

At least in my own personal purgatory.

"We could play with the laser pointer, or the scratching post that Ford brought home. You guys didn't need to buy that."

I shrugged as I stood up to put my weights away. I thought I saw her gaze rake over me, but that was probably wishful thinking. She only did that to Ford, and I did not blame her in the least. I did the same damn thing.

"Horatio is a new roommate. It's a gift."

"You guys have just been so great to me, everybody's been so great. Your family, Raven, Sebastian's family.

Everybody. Even Ford's brothers sent over dinner last night."

My lips twitched as I thought about that. I kept petting Horatio, mostly to do something with my hands so I didn't get up and do something horrible like hug Greer or something. "They wanted to come over here in full force, and that would have probably been too much for you."

Her eyes widened. "Seriously?

"Yep. He has a big family, just like I do. Though his are all brothers, rather than a shit ton of cousins like me. They didn't want to show up en masse and overwhelm. But I think they're only giving you a little bit of time before they show up and become as curious and invasive as my family."

"I wouldn't say your family's invasive," she said, defending the Montgomerys.

I shrugged, causing Horatio to jump off my lap.

With nothing for my hands to do, I turned slightly, feeling awkward just sitting there while Greer stood at the doorway. She looked down at Horatio, who looked up at her, then gently nudged against her calf before walking out of the gym.

Her shoulder sagged, and she let out a breath. "One day he'll let me pick him up. Not today, but maybe one day."

"I think at this point he's just doing it because he knows you love him and aren't going to give up."

"That's sweet. It's a big change, and I know he's doing well with you guys, and he sleeps with one of you every night, but I feel like I am always going to be fifth best or worst when it comes to him. But that's okay. He's my son and I love him."

I couldn't help it. She just looked so sad and lost, and I knew it had to do with more than just Horatio. I reached out and wrapped my arms around her shoulders. She stiffened for a moment before finally relaxing into my side and sighing.

"He usually sleeps with Ford. Not me. If that helps."

She laughed against me, and when she sniffled, I cursed.

"Don't cry. Horatio loves you. He doesn't hiss or anything when you're around."

This time her laugh was a little watery, and she wrapped her arms around my waist.

I ignored my need for her, because it was just ridiculous. I'd get over this quickly, just like I was getting over Ford, and I could be her friend. That's what she needed from me, not whatever attraction I had for her. It wasn't right for me to want anything more.

"Yes, he doesn't hiss at me, so I'm going to count that as a win. I guess. And how do you know he sleeps with Ford?" she asked, as she looked up at me.

There was a question in her gaze, one I didn't want to answer, so I just shrugged, my arm still around her shoulders. "Because he's not with me, and Ford always has cat hair over his bed now."

Greer winced. "I'm sorry. Seriously I'm so sorry. I should buy one of those things that I used to have for the upholstery. It worked wonders. I don't remember where I got it, but I'll find one."

"I know what you're talking about, and it's on our shopping list. You have a whole house to furnish, let us help with Horatio. It's the least we can do."

She pulled back and rubbed her temples. "I'm glad I have some things in storage like memory boxes, and clothes for other seasons. The rental was only a one bedroom with a large open space, but I still lost a lot, and my rental insurance is going to cover some of it, but not all of it. And with the landlords being jerks and doing weird things with the lease, I just don't know."

I narrowed my gaze, caught on the last part of her sentence. "What do you mean they are doing weird things with the lease?"

She stiffened before licking her lips. Once again, I didn't look at that action too hard. "They're waiting on the report from the fire inspector and police. If it's not faulty wiring, and if it's something else that they can blame me for, I think they're going to sue me. Or make me continue to pay rent to the end of my lease. I don't know what they can do, I don't know the legalities of it. But they're being jerks, and it's stressing me out, and I can't help but blame myself for burning down their damn house."

"First off, you didn't burn down their house."

"It feels like I did."

"You didn't. And you know what we're going to do? We're going to wait for the report, and then we're going to figure it out together. You forget, I work cybersecurity for a living, I can unearth anything. And the rest of our team? We've got you. We're not going to let them sue you or try to take out their anger on you. Fuck that."

"I just don't want to mess everything up. I feel like that's all I've been doing. And I haven't had a lot of time to even look for another place or find more clothes than what I've been able to borrow from Daisy and Raven and the other Montgomerys. All I've been doing is going from work to here and trying to sleep. That's it. And I just don't know how to thank you guys. You're letting me live with you."

"Of course we are. You're our friend. We weren't going to let you live out on the street."

She wiped her tears away, and I hated myself for making her cry. I never wanted to make her cry.

"I could have stayed with Raven or Daisy or someone else. But you're letting me stay here."

"Because you're our friend." And I needed to

remember that. She needed a *friend*, not someone who thought of her in any other way.

She nodded. "I'm going to head to bed. But thank you. For everything."

"Always." I paused, thinking what to say. "Ford should be home soon. He had to go work with one of his clients tonight on their security system."

"Do you guys usually work late nights? Doing stake-outs," she said, her voice teasing.

"That's not really our job. We're not PIs or cops. But if there's a problem with the security system that doesn't require the authorities, we have to go out and fix it. It's part of our guarantee. And Ford's been working with this client from the beginning."

A client that annoyed the hell out of me, and I knew was getting under Ford's skin, but I didn't put that out there. Greer didn't need to know.

"It's harder than making coffee, so I'm glad you guys are good at what you do and seem to enjoy it."

"You do realize I only know how to make coffee that comes in a pod?" I asked, being serious.

Greer shuddered before she winked. That wink did things to me that I didn't want to think about. "Don't worry, I'll help you with that."

"What, you don't like our pod machine?"

"The first things I'm going to buy for you guys when

I get the insurance money are a coffee maker and a grinder. Don't worry, I'll take care of you."

I wish you would.

I didn't say that out loud, either.

She met my gaze for a moment, and looked as if she wanted to say something, but instead she shrugged and went back down the hallway.

I watched her walk away, not knowing what to say, before I went back and finished my workout.

I needed to get this out of my system. I needed to do anything but think of Greer.

Her scream cut through my thoughts, and I dropped the weight quickly, running towards her room.

I slammed open the door, ignoring the fact that it'd been closed, and nearly fell to my knees.

Greer stood there, towel on the floor, her body naked and wet, as she stood at the outside of the bathroom door, eyes wide.

She must have dropped the towel, but I couldn't stop looking at her.

There was something wrong with me, and I needed to breathe. Needed to look away.

I needed to stop looking at her pert pink nipples, the way that they hardened under my gaze. Her breasts were large, bigger than my hands. They would overfill my palms, and I could imagine myself licking and sucking at her nipples, pushing my face in between them as I sucked in her essence, breathing and licking and sucking.

She had a thatch of brown curls between her legs, her pussy soft and swollen. Had she been touching herself in the shower? I wasn't sure, but all I wanted to do was put my hands on her wide hips and spread her thighs so I could taste that pussy.

She looked at me and I blinked before looking around.

"What's wrong? Why did you scream?"

Horatio took that moment to prance in beside me, before he lowered his head and pounced.

A mouse ran past me, Horatio on its tail, and I just stood there, frozen, as Greer stood naked.

"Let me guess, you found a mouse?"

"I think Horatio is getting it. But I really don't want him to eat that. I cannot believe I'm naked in front of you."

"I'm really sorry for barging in." I turned on my feet and covered my eyes, even though it didn't matter because I had already seen her.

I heard her behind me, pulling on her pants.

And now that I knew what her mound looked like, and the shape of her areolas, that was going to haunt me forever.

My God, I wanted to taste her. To see if she was sweet or tart. I wanted to push her over the bed, pull her ass up, and fuck her from behind. I wanted to see what her ass felt like around my cock, what her pussy felt like when it was clenching around me.

I willed myself not to think about that any longer, but my cock had other plans.

"I'm so sorry. I didn't mean to scream like a girl."

"You saw a mouse. I'm going to go catch it."

"Don't kill it."

I looked over my shoulder, grateful she was dressed.

"Are you serious?" I asked incredulously.

"It was a cute baby mouse, and I don't want Horatio to get sick eating it, either."

I cursed under my breath and followed the direction the cat went. However, Ford walked in the front door and caught Horatio before the cat ran out.

"I have no idea what just happened, but a mouse just ran out the front door. I take it Horatio was hunting?"

Horatio bumped his head on Ford's chin, and Ford stared at me, then behind me, at where I presumed Greer stood.

"You want to tell me what just happened?" he asked, as he looked pointedly down at my crotch, and then at a very wet Greer.

"Well, I saw a mouse, and then we took our next step as roommates because Noah just saw me naked. So now I'm going to die a little inside from embarrassment and go pet my cat."

I looked at Ford, and both of us burst out laughing.

Thankfully Greer joined in.

"I meant Horatio, not my pussy. And I'm going to stop saying pussy in front of you guys because now that one of you has seen my pussy, I feel like we've crossed a boundary."

Ford closed the door firmly behind him, then looked between us as he set Horatio down.

"I miss all the good things. We were getting naked and no one told me?"

I glared at Ford. "Don't start."

"What? Sounds kind of fun. I mean, you're both hot, so if it was going to happen, might as well happen when I'm home."

"You're a menace," Greer said, thankfully laughing.

"I'm just sad that I didn't get to see you naked first." Ford kept teasing, pushing, and I needed him to stop.

Because I didn't need to think about this any longer.

"Okay, now that you're making me laugh rather than feel embarrassed, I guess I'm grateful that we got that out of the way."

I blinked over at her. "What do you mean 'got that out of the way?'"

"I saw the way you looked at me, it's good to know." She shrugged, and I saw the bravado on her face was just a mask. Oh, she might feel it, but she was still embarrassed and stressed out about everything else.

There was something else, something I couldn't read on Ford's face, and that bothered me.

But before I could do anything about it, my phone buzzed and I looked down.

"It's a client. Looks like I have to go."

Ford just shook his head. "Saved by the call I guess," he mumbled, and I quickly shoved my feet into my outdoor tennis shoes, grabbed my wallet and keys, and headed out the door.

The two of them could handle whatever the hell was going on.

Because I sure as hell wasn't.

They'd be good for each other.

And I'd be good staying out of the way.

And not thinking about the fact that I had now seen both of them naked.

Chapter 5
GREER

THE AMOUNT OF PAPERWORK AROUND LOSING NEARLY everything felt like a slap in the face. I finally hung up the phone with another insurance agent and closed my eyes, telling myself that it would all be over soon. It had to be. There were only so many papers to sign. Right?

I didn't understand how there could be so much paperwork for a house that I didn't even own. But we were still waiting on the authorities, which didn't make any sense to me. How could they still not know after a couple of weeks? Surely, they didn't think I had done it.

"What's wrong?" Daisy asked from beside me. She had come into the back office to look over some paperwork, and though her office was only a couple of doors down in the building, it was nice to have some girl time.

At least that's how it had started, before we had both been on the phone.

"What?" I asked, my voice going only slightly high-pitched.

She smiled up at me and shook her head. "Are you okay? How is the insurance company?"

I gestured towards my notes. "I have no idea. I'm smart. I own a business with my best friend. I know what I'm doing most days. But they keep using words that make no sense, and it seems like they're contradicting themselves. We're still waiting on the damage report from the investigators, and the fact that they haven't explicitly said what started it worries me. Because they should know by now, right?"

Daisy nodded, as she fidgeted with her pen, the end tapping against the desk. "I'm sure they're just over-worked. We know that funding has been cut recently. Perhaps you're just on a list, and because it's not as damaging or scary as others, they'll get to you when they get to you."

I blinked at her. "You work in security. You literally help save people and protect them. And now you're just going in a roundabout way saying you have no idea why the authorities are giving me a runaround just as much as my insurance company."

Daisy winced, then shrugged. "Sorry. I don't really know what to say. It's weird though, but hopefully they'll get back to you soon and you can figure out what to do next." Daisy paused, seeming to contemplate what to say. "And then you can figure out if you're going to continue living with my cousin or find a place of your own."

I pressed my lips together. Daisy smiled at me, a wicked glint in her eye. Oh, Daisy wasn't upset that I was living with Noah and Ford, she was just curious. Just like the rest of them.

The Montgomerys were far more into each other's business than any family I had met. Ford claimed that his siblings were the same, though I hadn't met them yet. My brothers weren't nosy. It wasn't that they didn't care, it was that we didn't live near each other. We hadn't even when we were kids, so there had always been a distance and they couldn't be the overprotective brothers I thought I always wanted. Of course, in retrospect, seeing how the Montgomerys cared for their family, even if sometimes the connections were slightly frayed, made me think perhaps I hadn't wanted the overprotective brothers.

"I'm starting to look for a place, but the problem is because I am having trouble with the landlords and my current lease, including the insurance, I can't rent from anyone else. There's a huge red flag on my credit, and any references I'd have from prior living arrangements would not be good." And that hurt. Because I *was* responsible. I did what I was supposed to, and I worked hard. And now, due to something beyond my control, it felt like I was losing everything. Of course, perhaps it was my fault, and now this was my problem.

But no, I hadn't done this. I couldn't have.

"I still think that's bullshit, and you need to let us help you. You know we can look into it too."

I shook my head. "We already discussed this. There's no way I could afford you guys, and I'm not letting you do this pro bono. There is no way that I'm going to be in more debt to you and your family. The fact that the guys are letting me live there and refusing to let me pay rent is one thing. But I'm keeping track, and they're going to accidentally find money in their account one day. As soon as I get everything else settled."

Daisy grinned. "I can help you with that. After all, I'm the one that pays them from our accounts."

My eyes widened. "Really?"

"Of course. It used to be Noah, but then he started doing a thousand other things, and while he never dropped the ball, he also never slept. So we forced him to let us take some responsibility since we're all equal co-owners."

"I like the fact that you all work together. It's a big family thing."

"It can be a lot. The fact that I work with three of my male cousins means there's a lot of testosterone in the office. Add in Ford and Gus? Well, I'm just glad that I have Jennifer."

"I'm glad that you have her too. And you have the tattoo shop, and our café to help you with the estrogen."

"And thank the goddess for that," Daisy said with a wink. "Seriously though, thank you for letting me use your office. Noah and Ford and Kane are over there growling about one of their clients, and while I totally understand why, I wasn't in the mood to deal with it."

"And keep an eye on me because everybody's worried that I'm going to break down any minute."

I knew they were worried, but what else was I supposed to do?

"I haven't seen you break down yet, and neither has Raven."

I shrugged, my best friend working up front with the rest of our staff today. I was on paperwork duty, and my own personal paperwork. It sucked.

"I broke down during the fire. I freaked out and called Ford instead of 911. What the hell's wrong with me?"

"You were coughing, trying to get to your cat, and panicking. The fact that you were able to make a single call at all is a testament to how good you are in an emergency. Ford got the authorities there. If you're going to call anyone in an emergency, Noah or Ford are the ones I would recommend."

"I was a literal damsel in distress. It was not my best moment."

"My cousins have had my back more than once. And they've been damsels too. None of us are stereotypes. And that phrase is outdated anyway. You're allowed to let someone help you when you need it. That doesn't make you weak."

I studied my friend's face and I wondered why there seemed to be something she wasn't saying. But before I could ask about it, my phone rang.

"It's the detective I've been working with."

Daisy sat up and pulled out her phone.

I knew exactly who she was texting before I even had a chance to answer. I sighed and answered.

"Hello?"

"Hello, Ms. Cassidy? I have a few more questions for you."

I deflated in my seat. "You don't know what happened?"

"Oh, we have a guess. But we're going to need to talk to you down at the station."

I'd put my phone on speaker, so as Noah and Ford walked in, thanks to Daisy's text, they heard what he said.

"I'm sorry what?" I asked, my pulse racing.

"It's just some routine questions."

Before I could say anything though, Ford had the

phone in his hands, talking right into the receiver while keeping it on speaker.

"Hello, this is Ford Cage. I work with Montgomery Security. Is there something that we should be aware of?"

The man on the other end cleared his throat. "I remember you, Mr. Cage, and we have a few routine questions about the suspicious circumstances of the fire."

My hands shook as I took the phone back. This was *my* problem, and I was damn tired of everyone else taking control.

"I'm sorry what? What do you mean suspicious? I thought it was faulty wiring."

"Ma'am, we're going to need to ask you a few more questions, but right now it looks like the fire was set deliberately."

"Deliberately?" I asked, a ringing sound in my ears. "As in arson?"

"We just have a few questions, and we want to talk to you about them in person. We can meet you at your place of work if that would be better."

"How about you come to our offices," Noah said as he took the phone from me. I was getting really tired of that. I needed to do this on my own.

"We can do that. We like working with your team."

"Give me my phone back," I grumbled, stealing it

from Noah. "Who would do this? Why would somebody burn down the house?"

Nothing made sense. How could it? I didn't know anyone who would ever want to do that. It must have been an accident. Maybe someone was trying to burn down the house for my landlords? But that made no sense either.

"We'll meet you at the office in an hour."

He kept talking, the others answering for me, and I kept looking between them.

The detective finally hung up.

"Somebody tried to kill me? No, they just tried to burn down the house. Maybe they didn't know Horatio and I were inside." My palms went clammy, and it was hard to breathe. What the hell was going on? This didn't make any sense.

"Breathe, Greer. You're okay. You're safe. We're not going to let anything happen to you." Ford knelt in front of me, his hands covering mine. Noah stood behind him, arms folded over his chest as Daisy stood at his side.

These three were so strong, so capable, and here I was, nearly having a panic attack. I was not going to be that damsel. I could handle this. It had to be a mistake. And once I answered a few questions, everything would be fine.

"Do you have any idea who would want to do this?" Ford asked, his voice soft.

My gaze whirled to him, as anger and confusion warred within me. "Of course not. They have to be wrong. There is no way this fire was set deliberately. Who would do that?"

"You have an ex that you're worried about?" Noah asked, his voice soft. "Somebody who you might not remember from Portland? Maybe someone from school, or a customer?"

I shook my head. "Of course not. Yes, we have customers who sometimes don't like their coffee, but we deal with it. There's no way that a wrong coffee order is going to lead to someone burning my house down. And as for exes, the only guy I've dated here is Matt. And he was so passive that we weren't even a good fit. There's no way he would've burned down the house with me in it. He was a nice guy, he was just not my guy."

Ford looked over his shoulder at Noah, who was taking notes.

"Do not run a background check or wherever the hell you do on him. It wasn't him."

"You don't know that. But don't worry, we'll figure it out."

I rubbed my temples, taking my hands away from Ford's. "No. You guys don't need to take over. I can do this. I'm going to talk to the authorities, but I didn't do this. I have no idea who would. They have to be wrong."

"They're just going to ask some questions, and you're not going to be alone."

"We're going to figure this out," Noah growled, his voice deep.

I hated that I liked that growl.

It seemed like only yesterday I had been flirting with both of them, joking around because I was attracted to them, wanted them, but I had pushed those thoughts aside because the two of them just made sense together. I still thought that they made sense together, even though I didn't think they were actually seeing each other. But Noah had literally seen me naked yesterday, and I tried to laugh about it, but I couldn't get the thought out of my mind. Or the fact that I had seen his tented shorts, and my eyes had gone wide at that bulge.

All of that made much more sense, the attraction between the three of us, and the fact that we were all fighting it made much more sense than someone trying to burn down my house.

That had to be a mistake, just like me wanting the two of them was a mistake.

I stood up then, needing space. "I have a little bit of time before the authorities get here, and thank you for making sure it's at your office, rather than at the station. I don't want to deal with that. But I have to go back to work."

"Greer, you can take time off, it's okay," Ford said, his voice soft and soothing.

And I hated it.

"I will always be grateful to you guys for everything you've done, but I can handle this. I don't need you guys dropping everything all the time for me. Just, please, let me handle this."

Before they could say anything about the idiocy of me handling something like this when I had no idea what I was doing, and these three actually did it for a living, Raven walked in the back room and looked at everyone.

"Okay, clearly I've missed something." She gave me a pointed look. "And I'm sure you're going to tell me everything, because once again I'm left out of the loop. However, somebody sent you these and I thought you should have them."

I blinked and stared down at the small bouquet of primroses in her hand.

I frowned, oddly hesitant to take them. "What? Who sent me flowers?" For some odd reason, I turned to Noah and Ford, hoping it was one of them. But it wouldn't be, because Ford and Noah clearly weren't mine. I needed to get over this attraction.

But they just frowned, shaking their heads.

I didn't reach out for the flowers though, I couldn't, not when I had an odd feeling about them.

Raven looked between us, before Ford took the bouquet from her hands.

"Thanks, Raven, we've got this."

"Okay, clearly you don't, and you're going to explain it all." I walked with her out of the office.

Daisy cleared her throat. "I'll help."

"You don't have to do that, Daisy. You have a job of your own."

"And I can help my friends."

"And fill me in," Raven added, her voice serious. I nodded at both of them as they walked up front, leaving me alone with the guys. And I really didn't want to be alone with them right then, mostly because I had no idea what to think.

"Who's it from?" Noah asked.

"There's no note, just her name on the card," said Ford.

"I'm sure it's from a customer who liked their coffee, or one of the vendors I use. Or my brothers. I don't know. It's weird though. I can't think about it right now." I put the flowers on my desk and shook my head. "It's really, really weird, and I can't handle this."

Noah moved forward, cupping my cheek.

I swallowed, wondering why his touch made me burn. Noah always did his best not to touch me. I had noticed that right away. Ford always touched me, always hugged me, always took my hand. When we would walk through doors he'd gently place his hand on the small of my back to guide me. All little touches that I loved, but I knew I needed to stop craving. But Noah? He was so restrained. He only touched me when it looked as if he couldn't help himself. And yet here he was, cupping my cheek, and I knew if I let myself, I could give in. But I had to be strong.

I had to do this on my own, and not be so in debt I wouldn't be able to find my way out.

Because the worst part was that these guys felt sorry for me. It was why they let me live with them, it was why they were here now trying to help.

I didn't want to be a burden.

"You're our friend, Greer. And if something's hinky, we're going to figure it out. We're not going to take over," Noah said, and I scoffed.

"Okay, we might, we can't help it," Ford corrected. "But let us help. We're going to figure this out. And while you're getting on your feet, you do not have to ever think you're in debt to us. This is what friends do. I promise."

I sighed.

Friends. I could do this. I could rely on friends.

Because something was going on, something beyond an attraction between the three of us. Something was starting to worry me, and I had no idea what it was.

Chapter 6
FORD

WHEN I'D FINISHED COLLEGE AND HAD BEEN DECIDING between going into the military or starting a business with my best friend, I hadn't realized there would be so much paperwork. Seriously, the amount of paperwork that came with our job, the bureaucracy, red tape, and just signature after signature, made my brain hurt.

I knew that Noah and Daisy were better at it and could crank out an entire folder of paperwork in an hour when it took me at least two, but I wasn't going to lean on them for everything.

It wouldn't be fair, I had to pull my own weight.

So that was why Noah was gone for the day, having finished up his work with one of our clients, and was now working from home, probably so we wouldn't have to talk. Because ever since Greer moved in, things had been even more awkward than usual, and that was saying something, considering we had been walking on eggshells since the last time we'd been together. But that was a couple of months ago, and I was doing my best to ignore the fact that my best friend didn't want me that way. That I was a *distraction*.

Okay, enough of that. Noah was at home finishing up work, and I was here, trying not to bang my head against the computer.

"Why do you look like you want to scream?" Daisy asked from her desk. Kane and Kingston were also there, while Gus and Jennifer were on a job. They were providing security for an event, and the two of them worked damn well together. They had this *will they, won't they* vibe with each other, and I wasn't going to pry. No matter what happened between them, they didn't screw things up, or bring it with them into work like Noah and I did. Not that I thought that anyone knew what had gone on between Noah and me. It wasn't like I did either.

"I'm trying to fill out this last sheet, and I need a damn notary."

"I'm on it," Kingston said, as he pulled out a notary stamp from his desk.

I blinked at Noah's cousin. "When did you become a notary?"

Kingston beamed. "When I had to," he said with a

laugh. "Seriously though, I got things done. I know, shocking. What do you need me to sign?"

"This piece of paper for the government. I know, you're shocked," I said as I rolled my eyes.

We went over it together and Kingston did his notary thing. I shook my head. "Whose idea was it for you to become a notary? It was a damn good idea."

"Mine," Daisy said as she rubbed her fingernails on her shirt.

Kingston flipped her off, and she laughed.

"Let me guess, it was Noah's idea?" I asked, my voice dry.

"It's always Noah's idea," Kane said from the other side of the office, sipping coffee from Greer and Raven's coffee shop.

I brought my own coffee in that morning, because going in to see Greer was difficult enough. Although, I was using her coffee beans, and her coffee maker that she brought from her storage unit. So, technically, I was still using her coffee, I just wasn't staring at her awkwardly across the counter. Instead, I just stood awkwardly and stared at her across the island in our shared kitchen. That was perfectly fine.

"You doing okay?" Kingston asked.

"I'm fine. Just got a headache."

"If you're sure..." he said, drawing out the words.

I shrugged, then went back to work as the three of

them began talking about an upcoming event we were working security on. They were all cousins, some of them second cousins. Technically, Daisy and Kane were from the Colorado Springs branch, while Kingston was from the Boulder branch. Kingston and Noah had always been good friends, despite being four years apart. But that was probably because both of them were the children of poly relationships. They each had two dads and a mom, and grew up with the issues that came from society because of that. But I had always admired that to them it seemed normal, and when I was growing up with them, it became normal to me. And it should be. If you wanted a poly queer relationship, you should be able to have one. Of course, that made me think of a certain queer poly relationship I had in mind, but I wasn't going to let myself go there. That was just a recipe for disaster. Because it would just ruin everything. But I still had the idea in my head.

"Okay, let me get through this," Daisy said, running her fingers over her temples. "There's going to be five of us at this event,"

"You don't need Noah and me?" I asked, and Daisy shook her head.

"No, with the five of us we're fine. It's just a large charity event, and they don't want to bring in any additional outside private security."

"I'll work with law enforcement to make sure that

they know we'll be there, though," Kane said, as he took notes.

Like was evidenced with the fire, we had a good relationship with law enforcement. We weren't hunting down bad guys, or bounty hunters. We didn't go out and try to solve crimes. We just protected people who needed some extra security. We were all licensed to carry concealed in the state of Colorado and had valid permits. We were all retrained monthly. We had a gym at the back of the building where we worked out, and trained in take-down techniques to reduce the likelihood of having to use firearms. Our goal was to protect our people. We never wanted to escalate the situation, nor did we want to be in a position where we had to face the authorities on opposing ends. We hadn't yet, and damn it I refused to do that.

We provided security for events, we set up security systems for houses and businesses, we were bodyguards for certain people and for certain events. We went through security issues with new businesses and tried to find ways in and out. We had more contracts for that recently than we had in the past, which meant we would be hiring more people—like we had Gus and Jennifer— to make sure that we had the system for it. Noah was in charge of our cybersecurity, and that was more doing legal background checks for those that we were protecting and who we were protecting them from, as well as trying to test new businesses to make sure their data was secure. It was our job to think of the next step, to ensure that we knew what we were doing. Most of this had stemmed from Noah's father's business. And I liked that we still had him as our adviser, to make sure we weren't fucking up. The fact that so many of Noah's family members wanted to join the business always made me smile. My brothers hadn't, but I didn't mind. We each had our own lives.

Of course, that reminded me I had dinner with my family soon, because while I might spend more time with the Montgomerys, I was damn close to my brothers. Though they were exhausting sometimes.

My phone buzzed as I finished up my work and laughed when I saw the name.

"Hello, Aston," I said with a laugh to my eldest brother. "I was just thinking of you."

Aston's deep voice came on the line, his laugh a familiar part of my day. "It's like you're psychic or some shit. Hey, have you heard from Dad recently?" he asked, and I frowned.

"Not really. He was traveling with his buddies, and you know Dad. He gets weird sometimes."

"Yeah, that's what I thought. I was just going down the list of Cages to see what we're missing."

"You okay?" I asked, noticing an odd note in my brother's voice.

"Yeah, how about you? How's Greer doing?"

"She's doing fine. Well, I guess as fine as can be."

I moved from my desk to one of the private rooms in the back because I wasn't in the mood to get anyone's knowing looks when they heard Greer's name.

"I still think it's pretty damn cool what you're doing. And if you guys need anything, you'll let us know? Although at some point you're going to have to let us meet her."

I rolled my eyes even though my brother couldn't see me. "And why would I do that? She's my roommate."

"Yeah, and I hear the way that you talk about her. The same way Noah talks about her." There was a pause with so much meaning that I wanted to blurt everything. My brother was damn good at that, but I wasn't going to say anything. No, I needed to figure out what the hell I was doing first.

"You and Noah doing okay?"

"What's with the third degree? We're doing fine. As always."

"Well then, the whole 'as always' thing worries me, but I need to get back to work. However, we're going to meet Greer. I know that the Montgomerys stepped in first to help out and you didn't want to overwhelm her with forty of us added to that, but it's time. It's time to let the Cages in on the fun. The Montgomerys don't always get to be the saviors, you know."

"Is that bitterness I hear in your tone, dear brother?"

"No, just an annoying day that has nothing to do with the Montgomerys. I just want you to be okay."

"Of course, I'm okay." My phone beeped in my ear and I looked at the readout again, this time cringing. "Hey, I've got to go. It's my client."

"Stay safe, okay?"

"Always."

We ended the call, and I answered the next one, trying to keep my annoyance in check. This was a paying client, and she wasn't all that bad. But she was still exhausting. Not that I would ever admit to that out loud.

"Hello," she purred into the phone.

"Hello, Mrs. Price. What can I do for you?"

As soon as I said the words I knew I had left that too open. Jocelyn Price was a nice woman, but sometimes a little *too* nice. She was a little too touchy when working with some people. That's why I worked on this particular assignment, and not Gus, like originally planned.

She was recently divorced for the third time, and from what I could tell, was on the hunt for husband number four. Or at least boyfriend number seven, according to her. I was never going to be that, but I also had to go over to her house to help her with her security system and check for bugs every other week. It was getting annoying, and I knew I needed to nip this in the bud, but I wasn't about to admit to failure. I could deal with this. I had before. There were always those clients that wanted a little more hands-on security. It was like a drama for them, but I wasn't going to allow that to bother me. I was going to move on and deal with this.

"I'm having trouble, do you think you can help me?"

I sighed and agreed I'd be over there soon. I hung up and went to pick up my things.

"Everything okay?" Daisy asked.

I nodded. "Yeah. First my brother, now I have to go see Mrs. Price."

Both Kingston and Kane gave each other looks, and I ignored them. Daisy scowled, though. "I should be the one handling this."

"It's fine, I can do this. I've done this before."

"You shouldn't have to be sexually harassed because she's a client. We don't need her. And if she really needs a security system and help with it as much as she does, then I can handle it. Maybe bringing someone over without a penis will calm her down a bit."

I snorted and shook my head. "Me and my penis can handle it." I paused. "Not that I'm going to use my penis —let's pretend I never said any of that."

I ignored Kane and Kingston practically falling out of their chairs from how hard they were laughing. Daisy gave me a sad look. "Okay, I know you can handle it, but I don't want you to."

"I've got this. I always do."

She shook her head, but didn't stop me. I was grateful, because frankly I wasn't sure that I could deal with it right then. But I headed over to Mrs. Price's, and hoped to hell I wasn't making a mistake.

BY THE TIME I got home, I was exhausted. Not just from work, but from fending off Jocelyn Price. She was past being subtle at this point, and I didn't want to deal with it anymore. Nor did I want to have to tell Daisy she was right. I had already made a note in the client's file, and I had a feeling that once we sent Daisy in, either everything would stop, or Mrs. Price would no longer be our client. The fact that the woman had touched my ass not once but twice trying to walk past me, made me not care either way.

I got home, noticed Greer's car wasn't in the garage, and assumed that she was closing for the night.

We still didn't know who had burned down her house, or had sent those flowers. And while she said she could handle it, I knew Noah was on it. There was no way he wouldn't be. And as soon as I could think again, I would be right beside him, helping him figure it out.

But first, I needed a fucking drink.

The office door was closed in the back, so I assumed Noah was working, so I went to the kitchen and poured myself a glass of whiskey. I didn't usually drink it straight like this, but damn it, today required something more than just beer.

I took a sip, letting it settle on my tongue before I swallowed, the smokey flavor exactly what I needed.

I hated everything going on in my head. It was all too much, and I couldn't weave all the threads together. It was like everything was falling out of my hands, slipping between my fingers, and I wasn't strong enough to fix it. I knew what I had to do. I had to just talk to him. If I talked to Noah, figured that shit out, maybe things wouldn't be so painful.

I snorted and took another sip of my whiskey. Oh yeah, because me talking to Noah would totally help things out. Just like it had before.

"Bad day?" Noah asked from where he appeared on the other side of the kitchen, leaning against the doorway. He had on a tight black shirt and jeans that molded to his ass. When he folded his arms over his chest, his muscles bulged. I knew that Noah hadn't dressed like this on purpose, it was just comfortable for him, but I knew those jeans, they were well-worn, faded at the ass and the knees. They were soft against my hands, I knew, because I had peeled them off of him.

Just like I had peeled that shirt off him before. I had licked every inch of him, had touched all those muscles, and kissed and craved.

There was something wrong with me, and I needed to stop wanting my best friend. The problem was, it wasn't just want or desire. I *loved* my best friend. It was a fucking problem.

"I was over with Jocelyn," I said after a minute, before I downed the rest of my whiskey. I went to pour another glass, but Noah came forward and put his hand on mine. I froze, his hands so damn warm, rough, and calloused. I'd had those hands on my body before, and I wanted them there again. But I wasn't going to. Because if I did, it would just be another mistake, like he said before. But this time it wouldn't be Noah running from his problems. It would be me.

But maybe it was my turn.

"Are you okay? Did she hurt you?"

"Really? She's the size of my pinky. She didn't hurt me."

"I would say size doesn't matter, but we're not going to go down that path," Noah said with a dry laugh.

I rolled my eyes and moved my hand back so I could reach for another glass. I poured us both two fingers of whiskey, before clinking my glass to his and taking another sip, this time slower. Noah met my gaze as he sipped too.

"Seriously. You okay?"

"I'm fine. I think Daisy's going to take her next time,

and if that doesn't work, we're going to need to dump her as a client."

"I told you to dump her as a client two ass-pinches ago."

I winced and set the glass down. "It's been a long fucking day." I paused and looked at the front door. "Greer still at work?"

"She has inventory with Raven tonight. Said she'd be late. You want me to order something for dinner? Or I guess we can make something. I think we have enough vegetables for some kind of stir-fry."

"Maybe. I don't know, I'm having a weird day."

There was nothing really weird about it, other than I was standing alone in the kitchen drinking with Noah, and all I wanted to do was reach out and touch him. So when Noah reached out and cupped my face, I froze. Because Noah didn't touch me anymore.

"Talk to me, Ford," he whispered.

"It's damn hard to do that when you're touching me like this."

"So, no talking."

"Okay."

This was such a fucking mistake, but damn it, I loved him. And I was so tired of pretending I didn't. Noah leaned forward and brushed his lips against mine. I let him, I just fucking let him.

It started off sweet, soft, his tongue gently brushing

against my lips. But when I opened for him, it went deeper, darker.

We'd slept together for the first time years ago. We liked being with one another, but we always said we'd put our friendship and our business first. We hadn't wanted to mess things up. And I wanted to believe that was enough for me. Just like I believed it was enough now.

He kissed me harder, and I pulled at his shirt. He laughed against me as he lifted his hands up and I pulled his shirt over his head, tossing it over the counter.

He bit at my lip, then kissed my chin, my neck. He tugged off my shirt, as both of us worked on our jeans, laughing as we stumbled out of the kitchen. We needed lube, and we weren't going to find it here.

We fell on the bed, on top of each other as we shucked off our jeans, both of us in boxer shorts rubbing against one another.

He was hard, the tip of his dick poking out of his underwear.

I slid my finger over the slit, rubbing pre-come around. He groaned, rocking his hips into my hold. I fisted him, pulling him completely out. I wiggled down the bed before licking him, taking the tip of his cock into my mouth. He groaned, sliding his hands into my hair.

"There you go, swallow me."

I hummed against him as I cupped his balls. I was

practically dry humping the bed as I went down on him, swallowing him so the tip of his dick reached the back of my throat. I relaxed my throat, letting him go impossibly deeper. He was big, wider than me, but not as long. We had always joked about that, comparing when we were drunk. But that was who we were, dumbasses who wanted each other.

When he tugged on my hair, I knew he was going to go, so I let him, swallowing him as he came down my throat, the salty musky taste almost enough to nearly send me over the edge.

I pulled away and licked my lips before I crushed my mouth to his, wanting him to taste himself on my tongue.

"You're so fucking hot with my dick in your mouth."

"Yeah? Bend over so I can see what my dick looks like in your ass, that's exactly what I need."

"You say the sweetest things."

We continued to kiss, to explore. I open the bottle of lube, preparing him and myself. But he didn't go down on his knees at first. He just continued to pet me, getting me impossibly harder.

This was the Noah that I loved. The rough one who turned sweet. Because he put everyone first no matter what, which was why I made sure he came first.

I finally put him on his knees so we faced the end of the bed, and I positioned myself.

"Are you ready?"

"I've been ready since I saw you suck down that whiskey."

I laughed, and then I moved forward.

We both groaned at the sensation, his ass tightening around my dick. He was tight, and I had to go slow. We might pretend we liked it rough, but I never wanted to hurt him.

He moved back against me, his ass against my hips, and I pumped, thrusting in and out of him. We both moved, sweat slick, groaning, and when I finally came, he did again, spurting over the bedsheets. I kissed up and down his back, my body shaking, as I finally relaxed and tried to catch my breath.

When Noah froze beneath me, I looked up and froze right along with him.

Greer stood there, eyes wide and mouth parted.

Well…things just got complicated.

Chapter 7
NOAH

THIS WASN'T QUITE A NIGHTMARE, BECAUSE I HAD pictured this in my mind before. Greer walking in on us just like I had walked in on her. I knew the exact color of her nipples, the way her pussy looked as she pressed her thighs together. I had those images in my dreams, though not consciously, because I always did my best not to think about her like that. But when I was asleep? My dreams did whatever the fuck they wanted to.

We knelt there on the bed, staring at Greer, no one wanting to speak first.

Then Greer slapped her hands over her eyes and whirled around, nearly falling into the doorframe.

"I'm so sorry... I didn't realize... I'm going to... Well, I don't know what I'm going to do. I don't want to wash my eyes with bleach or anything, but oh my God. I'm so sorry."

She moved to the right, ran straight into the wall, shook herself off, then kept going, looking between her fingers so she wouldn't hit the wall again.

My fingers dug into the duvet and I cleared my throat. "I think we need to start moving."

Ford's hands gripped my hips, and for a second I thought he'd move deeper inside me, instead he slid out, the sensation oddly freeing and hot at the same time.

I rolled onto my back and ran my hands over my face as Ford knelt in front of me, shaking his head.

"Let's clean up, and then go see what the hell we need to do."

"I can't believe we didn't close the door," I muttered.

"True. There're a lot of things I can't believe we just did after saying we wouldn't, but for right now let's go make sure we didn't traumatize our roommate." Ford frowned at me. I didn't know what else he was going to say, or what he could say. I wasn't always the asshole in this relationship. We used to switch it off, taking turns on who was the growly one. But recently, only I was the asshole. Ford was the one cleaning up my messes, trying to find humor in any situation. I thought he should be with Greer, I figured they would be a good match because the two of them got along. They just seemed to click.

But instead, I lay here underneath my best friend, not boyfriend, and sighed.

"I don't want to hurt her."

Ford looked down at me and frowned again, that little V between his eyebrows deepening.

"Why do you think we would hurt her?" he asked, his voice soft.

"Because I'm really good at hurting you." And with that honesty I hadn't planned on saying at all, I rolled off the bed and headed to the bathroom. I didn't say anything else, just quickly cleaned up and stuffed myself back in my jeans, searching for my T-shirt along the way. Ford had gone back to his room and I heard the shower running. I wasn't sure what I was supposed to do. I hadn't heard the front door, nor had any of the security alerts gone off saying she left, but then again, we hadn't heard our phones go off when she entered the house. We had been too lost in each other. And perhaps that was the problem. I was so in my head when it came to Ford, and now maybe Greer, that I was losing time. I was messing up, just like I had before, when we almost lost Raven.

My chest ached and I ran my hand over my heart, annoyed with myself.

People had almost died because I hadn't known who Wyatt was. It didn't matter that he hadn't had a record, that he hadn't shown any warning signs. I should have seen it. There had to have been signs, and I hadn't seen them.

And Wyatt, the man who had run his own business out of a building our family owned, had slipped past all of us and hurt one of ours.

Our family had been hurt.

So no, I wasn't going to forgive myself very easily. Especially when my distraction these days meant that I was also hurting the people that I cared about the most.

I wasn't sure when Greer had joined that number. And I wasn't sure I wanted to look deeper into that.

Because, like Ford, she was my roommate, and I was going to hurt her if I wasn't careful.

But damn it, I wasn't sure what I should do. Ford would know, and I would follow his lead. Because Ford always knew.

Especially when I didn't.

I made it to the living room and saw Greer pacing there mumbling under her breath.

"Hey," I said, not sure what else to do. I didn't want to just stand there watching her without her knowing I was there.

She whirled, her cheeks blushing to that pretty pink as she pressed her lips together.

"Oh, hi. I probably should have knocked or something."

I burst out laughing, I couldn't help it. This was all just so insane.

She tilted her head. "I have no idea what's so funny, but I might just join you in the insanity." Her lips twitched.

I waved her off. "I'm sorry. But come on, in less than a week, I've walked in on you naked, and well, I guess you walked in on me in a slightly more prone position."

She was silent for so long I was afraid I had gone too far, before she burst out laughing.

"Oh, you were prone all right," she said, wiping away tears.

I grinned, grateful that some of the tension seemed to be gone. Well, not all of it. No there was that familiar tension when it came to Greer. But that was on me and the fact that I couldn't get over this attraction to her. I needed to; I would be better off if I did.

"Well, laughter is a soothing way to start a conversation like this," Ford said as he walked into the living room barefoot. He'd put on jeans and a T-shirt, and his hair was wet. He pushed it from his face, the wet strands sliding over his eyes, and he gave me one of those half-smiles that always did something to me.

I hadn't always been in love with my best friend. He'd had lovers, boyfriends, and girlfriends over the years, just like I had. We had gone our separate ways for college, at least in terms of our disciplines, but we were still roommates. We owned the house together now.

Our lives were irrevocably tangled, and one drunken night we had fallen into bed with one another. It was our own toxic attraction that kept us coming back for more, but perhaps it would have been better if we hadn't.

"I just want to say that I'm so sorry for interrupting you two. That was none of my business, and I really shouldn't have stared for as long as I did."

"We left the door open," I said dryly. "That's on us."

Greer cleared her throat and pointed to a T-shirt that lay over a lamp. "I guess I should just be glad that you didn't finish here where it seems you started."

Ford sighed and reached over to pluck the T-shirt off the lamp. "I was wondering where that went."

I rubbed my temple. "You know, I have no idea how to begin this conversation. How does one begin a conversation for something like this? We've already had the apology where I walked in on you naked. And now here we are."

"Again, you thought you were saving my life. From a mouse. That my cat decided to chase." She paused and looked around. "Where is my cat?"

"He was sleeping in the sunroom," Ford answered. "I guess, uh, we were a little loud for him." This time it was Ford who blushed, the tips of his ears going red.

That was so damn sexy, and it had taken me a long

time to learn to hide my reaction. Because Ford wasn't mine. I just really hoped that whatever just happened didn't ruin things for him and Greer. It would be good for both of them. And as soon as I got over myself and actually walked away from them, they could begin, and things would make sense.

Greer rocked on her heels, looking damn cute with nerves. "I am sorry for walking in on you guys. But really, maybe we should have a closed-door system. We all have separate rooms so we don't need a sock on the door, but maybe the door doing what a door does so you can't see through the door would be great." She paused. "I think I just said the word door like fourteen times. I have no idea why I'm so flustered. Oh wait, it's because that might have been the hottest thing I've ever seen in my life, and now I keep imagining it, and it's really rude because I shouldn't be fantasizing about my roommates going at it. The fact that you guys haven't told anyone else about your relationship tells me that this is something between the two of you and now I'm encroaching on it, and I really need to stop talking."

I stood motionless, trying to catch up with her words, but Ford moved forward.

"Again, you don't need to apologize, and yes you did use the word door a few times, but maybe we should actually use one." Ford smiled at me.

I shrugged. "I was distracted."

"I'll say," Greer mumbled, then put her hand over her mouth again.

She mumbled something through her fingers. Ford sighed before gently tugging on her wrist.

"What?"

"Oh nothing. I'm just thinking about things I shouldn't think about."

That's when I noted the blush on her cheeks that had nothing to do with being embarrassed. Interesting. Very interesting.

"Noah and I are friends. Best friends."

I cleared my throat. "And roommates, and everything else in between. We don't have a label per se. More of a *situation*."

Ford glared at me. "Maybe we should have a label," he snapped.

I froze, realizing I had stepped in it. "We haven't needed one before," I said slowly.

"Well, maybe it's fucked up that we don't."

"You guys...I shouldn't. I really shouldn't be here," Greer said, then she looked down and realized that Ford was still holding her hand. Where the hell was Ford going with this? I had an uneasy feeling he was doing something that was going to change everything, but damn it, I trusted him. Maybe I would let him take the leap. I would follow his lead because I sure as hell didn't know what to do next.

"With the way you're looking between us, I have a feeling you liked what you saw?" Ford asked, his voice soft.

I pressed my lips together, holding back a smile, because Greer looked like she wanted to melt into the floor. "Ford. Are you really going to grill her?"

"I just have questions. You don't have to answer anything, Greer. But I saw the way that you looked at us, and I remember what you said before when Noah decided to walk in on you naked."

I looked at Ford. "I didn't decide to do it, it happened accidentally." Greer frowned, and I quickly continued. "Not that I actually regret it because, well, I should just stop talking right now. Now I get why you were rambling."

It was my turn to blush. Greer smiled, and Ford had a look in his eyes that scared me, but I didn't say anything.

"Like Noah said, we have a situation. Perhaps it would be better with labels, but that's something that we've been working on." Ford looked at me for a moment, before turning back to her. For some reason I wanted to stop him. I wanted to make sure he didn't say what I thought he was about to...and yet I knew I needed him to. "But Greer? We both want you too."

Greer stood silent, the profoundness of it hitting me like a two-ton truck.

I honestly couldn't believe Ford had just said it. But then again, it was how we had made it work the first time with us, for at least a short time. But this was Greer and things were different.

Her mouth fell open and she blinked between us. "What? Oh. Well. Thanks. I again have no idea what to say."

Damn it, Ford was putting it all out there, I couldn't let my best friend do it alone. I might as well throw myself over the cliff with him. "He's right, you know. I'm bi, and want you too. But I didn't want to be weird about it."

Greer's mouth parted. "Oh... Oh... Well..." She moved back, rubbing her hands over her face. "This is the most awkward conversation, and yet not an awkward conversation at the same time." She looked between us. "I dated Matt, and others, even though I really wanted you both from the first moment I saw you, and I knew it was wrong because I thought you were perfect for each other. And oh my God. I can't believe I'm actually having this conversation. With both of you. I never really wanted to choose which of you I liked more, and though there are many poly relationships in our lives, I've never actually been in one so I didn't know how to go about that. And then I just thought you two were together, even though no one else really did, and now I'm just going to shut up."

Ford was so much better at this than me, taking a risk I felt like I couldn't, but if he could, so could I. Something was going on here, something that could blow up in our faces, but if Ford wanted this, then maybe I would let myself finally want it too.

"What are you talking about?" she asked after a few moments passed where neither of us spoke up.

"I'm talking about maybe the three of us trying something." Ford paused. "I'm not asking you to bed." At both mine and Greer's sounds of confusion, Ford continued. "I mean, that would be great, but maybe we could try to date. The three of us."

"Date. The three of us. Don't you think that would be a bad idea?" I asked, and I ignored the hurt on Ford's face to look at Greer. "It's just—I don't want to hurt you. I'm really good at hurting people. Ask Ford. It's all I seem to do."

Compassion slid over her face, and she stepped forward. I didn't stop her when she grabbed my hand and squeezed. "I think you're punishing yourself, but I don't know why. I'd like to know why, so that way I can snap you out of it. You're not a bad person, Noah."

"I'm a bad bet."

"And I'm great at bad ideas." Her lips twitched as she said it, and Ford stepped toward us.

"I'm also great at bad ideas. And Noah? I think you

getting out of this house and actually being seen with me in public? That could help."

"Ford, it's not that. You know I'm not ashamed of you. You're my best friend and I don't want to ruin that." I looked at Greer. "And I like you, too. You're my friend, now my roommate. You're going through so much."

"I can still make my own decisions. I can't say I haven't thought about it, the three of us. I just haven't let myself think too seriously."

"If we do this, what if we fuck everything up? What if we ruin it all?" I didn't know when I had become the voice of caution. "So there's attraction between us, we all know this, you happen to walk in on us, and now we're all saying that we want to go out on a fucking date?" I asked incredulously.

Greer looked down at her hands and shrugged. "Maybe I'm dreaming, and this is the beginning of a really bad porn."

"There's nothing bad about a porn we would be in," Ford said, and I glared at him.

"This isn't funny. We could ruin everything."

Ford was in my face then, hand behind my neck. I swallowed hard, the familiar touch nearly sending me over the edge once again. "You don't screw things up. You don't *talk* about things, and that can screw things up, but you existing? No, you don't fuck it up. Maybe we should actually do something about the tension between the three of us because it's always been there. We've been hiding it since she first opened up the coffee shop, so let's try something. As long as we're open and honest, we won't fuck it up. But you have to talk, Noah. I'm not going to hurt you, and I'm not going to lose you. Same with Greer."

He stepped back, allowing Greer to come between us. "I can walk away right now. I don't want to interrupt anything."

And from the hurt in her voice, I knew I was already fucking this up. I cursed under my breath, and then cupped her face. She blinked at me. "I've wanted you, Greer. We've both wanted you. And we've done our best not to think about it. I get it though. We're not good at talking about what we want, because we always think we know what's better for the other person. So let's try this. Let's see if this works. But I don't want to hurt you. I don't want you to feel like you're in the middle of something, either. This is where we start fresh. Where we finally give in. But the moment you need to walk away? You do it. The moment you need me to stop standing between the two of you? You tell me."

"You're an idiot," she whispered, and I tilted my head in surprise.

"What?"

"You're not standing in the way, Noah. If anything, I thought I was."

"And this is why we're going to talk. We're going to just go out to dinner. Get a beer, figure out if this is something we all want."

We both turned to Ford who shrugged.

"I'm tired of tiptoeing. I'm tired of pretending I don't want you both. And yeah, we could screw this up, but what if we don't? What if we get exactly what we want?"

I cleared my throat and nodded. "Okay. Just a date. Just to see. No promises."

"Just a date, the only promise is not to hide when things get tough. Because that's what I'm good at."

I looked at her then and knew there was something beneath the surface. Something I wanted to know.

I nodded, agreeing to a single date. No labels, no situations. Just a date.

I knew this was a damn mistake, but maybe for a moment, I could pretend. Maybe for a moment, I could let myself believe.

Chapter 8
GREER

"WHAT WAS I THINKING?"

I paced my bedroom, looking at the meager clothing options I had. After all, most of my clothes had been burned less than a month ago. I'd kept many of my memories, furniture, and kitchen items in storage, but not my clothes. The authorities were still trying to figure out exactly what had happened, and they still weren't saying if it was arson or an accident. They just didn't know, and that meant I couldn't move on. I couldn't use insurance money to find a new place, couldn't buy new outfits, couldn't get a new full cat tree for Horatio. I could do none of that until things were settled.

And yet none of that mattered right then because I needed to figure out what I was going to wear tonight.

"I brought over everything that I could, but we're not

exactly the same size or body shape, but Lake also gave me a few things," Raven said, mentioning Sebastian and Noah's cousin.

"Lake is beautiful and slender and has perfect boobs. I'm not going to be able to fit in anything she owns."

Raven lifted a brow and shook her head. "Really? You guys are the same height, have the same size hips, and you also have beautiful boobs. You might have to stuff your boobs into whatever low-cut dress she gave you, but you're not going to a place that requires a dress, right?"

I ran my hands over my face again and continued to pace. "We're going to a brewery. To try beer and eat pretzels and for me to get completely bloated, which doesn't really matter because I like the way I look. I don't even know why I'm complaining. I think it's the fact that I only had two cups of coffee today."

"You have an issue when it comes to caffeine."

I narrowed my eyes at my best friend. "So says the woman that went into business with me. We have an equal addiction to caffeine, specialty coffees, and every kind of baked good that you're a goddess at. See these boobs." I pointed to my breasts, and Raven beamed.

"Oh yes, I've seen your boobs. I'm looking at them right now in your bra."

"Well, these boobs got bigger when I started working

with you. As did my ass. But that's fine. Like I said, I like the way I look. But we have an addiction."

"And from what I'm hearing, Noah and Ford also like the way you look. So I guess they should thank me for your boobs."

I sputtered, shaking my head. "I have no idea how we got onto this conversation."

"Because you're pacing around in your bra and panties in your bedroom, trying to figure out what you're going to wear."

"What am I doing?" I asked as I shoved on a top and tried to see if it matched anything. It was a lacy black top that wasn't too formal, but still sexy. I could probably pair it with jeans and cute black-heeled sandals. That would be fancy and yet casual enough for a brewery. And I had that hot leather jacket that could work with it.

Outfit decided, I got dressed, but realized that Raven hadn't answered.

"Earth to Raven? What am I doing?"

"Right now, you're bending over in just underwear in front of me as you pull on your jeans."

"Oh stop it," I said, as I wiggled my jeans over my ass. "Seriously. Why did I actually decide to do this?"

"Because you've been lusting after them since we first started working next to them."

I paused in the act of buttoning my jeans. "You noticed?" I asked, my voice going high-pitched.

"I'm your best friend, of course I noticed."

"You don't think anyone else did, do you?"

"No, except maybe in the way that everyone looks at them because they're hot."

"You're with Sebastian. Should you be noticing that they're hot?"

"Of course I'm allowed to notice they're hot. I'm not going to do anything about it. Dork. And they are hot. And I've noticed them checking you out. I just never thought that you guys would actually do something about it."

"I wasn't expecting this."

"Then have fun tonight. You're allowed to have fun, Greer. You've been through so much."

"But what if I ruin it?"

"You won't. You're being open. You're going to have fun. This is just a date."

I ran my hand over my stomach, looking at myself in the long mirror. "But they're already sleeping together. And I didn't even ask them about it when this whole date thing came up. We just fell into conversation about other things, and I didn't actually point out the fact that they're already together and I'm just sliding right into it. Things are weird, and I just, I just said yes because my life is falling apart, and while my fantasies and fanfics have been about this exact scenario, I didn't actually think it would happen."

"There was a lot in that sentence, but you know what? Find out what's going on between them. If they're inviting you into what they have, you have a right to ask."

"I don't know. I don't want to ruin everything."

"You can't ruin anything by asking. By talking." Raven paused, her attention on my duvet as she picked at a loose thread. "Or just have fun tonight, and not do anything serious and just enjoy the evening. Be safe and be careful. And I love you."

I strode over to my best friend and hugged her tightly.

"I love you so much. And you're right. It's just a date. It's just dinner. I've had dinner with them countless times already, either with all of the Montgomerys, or at the house I live in with them. This is totally not complicated," I lied.

Raven just raised a brow again before kissing my cheek. "I'm going to head out before they come and pick you up."

"You mean pick me up from the room that is two doors down from Noah's and then another door down from Ford's? Because this isn't weird at all."

"It's like dorm living. You're fine."

"We keep saying I'm fine, but I feel like we don't understand what that word means."

Raven shook her head and left me standing there, wondering if I was making a mistake.

Knowing that I really was.

I turned to put the rest of my clothes away and scratched Horatio under the chin. The fact that he let me was surprising, but I didn't have time to dwell on that because there was a knock on the door frame.

"You ready to go?" Ford's deep voice asked, and I turned, nearly tripping in my sandals.

He stood there in dark jeans that molded to those thick thighs that I loved and tried not to stare at. He had on a Henley, rolled up to the elbows. I loved when guys did that, and I hated it. Because then I had to stop staring at their forearms. Why were forearms sexy? I didn't know. It was a kink of mine, just like hands. Because I really liked Ford's hands.

I finally looked up at his face as his eyes lit up. "You look damn sexy, Greer. I hope it's okay that I said that."

"I was just lusting after your forearms, so I think we're even." I quickly shut my mouth, as Ford threw his head back and laughed.

"What did I miss?" Noah asked, when he came to stand by Ford. Noah wore a white button-up shirt over jeans, his sleeves also rolled up to his elbows. Noah had ink on his forearms, done by Leif if I remembered correctly, and I sighed happily.

I hadn't realized I did it out loud until Ford grinned like he knew all the secrets in the world.

"Greer was just lusting after my forearms, and she nearly swooned looking at yours. I guess we're going to have to compare later."

Noah looked down at his arm, then at Ford's, before looking at me.

"Forearms? That's good to know."

I quickly grabbed my bag and shook my head. "Like you two don't know. You're into each other, you've noticed your…each other's forearms."

Noah winked. "Maybe we have. Come on, we can all hop into my SUV, and we'll head to the brewery. I haven't been to this one, but I've always wanted to try it."

"Are you sure a family member doesn't own it?" I asked, and Noah laughed.

"No. And it's not a Cage Brothers one either."

"Your family owns businesses too?" I asked.

Ford shrugged as he helped me into the front seat. "We have Cage Enterprises. Well, my brothers do, we sort of work for them. Long story."

My eyes widened.

"As in the huge real estate developer that is actually environmentally conscious?" I asked, thinking of the multimillion, probably billion-dollar company.

"Yep. We're taking over the world, we're just not as massive as Noah's family is."

"And don't even get me started on one of my dad's families. We just sprawl out all over everywhere," Noah said as Ford closed the door. He started the engine as Ford hopped into the backseat.

"I could have sat in the back you know. You guys have longer legs than me."

"Your legs are just fine," Ford said as he settled in.

"I'd say more than just fine, but again, I'm not trying to compete here."

I just laughed as we fell into conversation about work and Horatio. This was easy, it's what we'd always done. It didn't feel awkward until we sat down at our table at the brewery. I sat between them, feeling the heat of them. We all ordered beers, and a pretzel with hot mustard as an appetizer. I didn't know what to say, but the conversation turned to favorite movies. I figured maybe I should ask what I should have at the beginning.

"Okay, now that we've discovered your favorite James Bond was Sean Connery," I said as Ford sputtered and Noah rolled his eyes, "I have a couple questions that I probably should have asked before we got here and started on our first beers."

Noah tapped my half-finished beer. "You're not at all drunk yet, so ask what you want."

We sat in a back booth, one a little more secluded so

no one would be able to hear us. When the waitress came back to hand off our pretzel and take the rest of our order, I was grateful for the reprieve so I could think.

"I know this is a date and I know we're trying to figure things out, but are you together? Am I intruding? Am I just...fun?"

Noah tapped my shoulder, and I turned my attention to him. "We aren't together," Noah answered, and Ford cursed under his breath.

I looked between them, feeling awkward as hell, as Noah sighed.

"We're in a situation." Ford repeated Noah's words from earlier.

"It's complicated," Noah answered again.

"And I'm just going to make this worse, aren't I?" I said quietly, feeling as though I needed to escape, but I couldn't since we were in a U-shaped booth and the only way out would be to crawl under the table and call a car service or Raven to get me home. Home, where I lived with the two of them.

This was so beyond idiotic.

"You're not going to make this worse," Noah said.

"We're on a date. We're having fun."

I looked at both of them and shook my head. "We should talk about it."

"Then we will. When we go home. We'll finish our meals, talk about everything else, and when we get home, we'll talk about what this means. But let's enjoy this date first."

"Just talk?" I asked, my voice low.

"Just talk," Noah agreed readily.

I saw the look between them and knew that we needed to. But if we did, we'd shatter the impossibly fragile bubble that we were already in.

It wasn't enough. I knew that this would end quickly, and I didn't want it to yet. So I changed the subject.

I took a big bite of the pretzel and grinned. "Favorite restaurant. Go." Ford looked relieved and Noah began to play with my hair.

"Well, that's going to take some time."

BY THE TIME we got home, I was warm and happy and full. We'd each only had the one beer, that way we were safe to drive home, and the sense of anticipation had flowed over all of us.

It was weird, and yet exactly what I wanted.

It was nice, though I knew that once we stepped inside and spoke, it could all fail.

Or I could take a leap that I wasn't prepared for but craved.

"So," I said softly as we sat on the couch, none of us touching, but close enough I could still feel the heat of them. I'd had such a great time, I didn't want it to end.

But I knew if we did anything else beyond this, or if we just walked away, we needed to get through this one part.

"Noah and I are best friends who like to enjoy each other." Ford shrugged. "But what we just did? That was our first date."

"Fuck no it wasn't," Noah blurted. "Was it? I mean, between the two of us. That was a first date between the three of us, but, Ford, we've been on a date, haven't we?"

I stared between them, a little shocked, and yet happy. I liked the way the two talked to one another and still included me. I had never been on a threesome date before, and I didn't know the rules, but maybe the rules were just talking it out, and that's what we were doing.

"It was," Ford said with a laugh. "But it seems right that it was with Greer, you know?"

"But I thought we went on dates. At least, the two of us?"

"No, that was always as friends and roommates. But dating? We keep that to the bedroom."

I reached out and gripped Ford's hand and he smiled softly down at me. "It's okay. Like I said, that situation was and is something that we're dealing with together—with the three of us. Because it doesn't seem right to leave you out of this conversation."

"But I thought we went out with Cynthia?" Noah blurted as Ford sighed.

I froze. "Who is Cynthia?" I asked, an odd feeling in

my gut. Both men gripped my hands and squeezed, and I could breathe again.

"Cynthia was someone that we thought could work with us. We went out dancing with Cynthia once, and we fought, twice. It didn't work. She didn't want us. She wanted the show, and then she wanted to laugh about it later. It didn't work out the way we wanted. But the three of us, with *you*, Greer, I like it, and I want to do it again. I'm tired of fucking walking around on eggshells about it."

I just sat there, as frozen as Noah. When Noah reached out and settled his hand on my knee, I knew he was needing comfort. So I gripped his hand and squeezed.

"That was a lot."

"Yeah, it was," Ford whispered.

I looked at Noah, who swallowed hard. "For a first date, I'm glad it was us three."

And right then and there, my heart burst. I didn't know what that meant, didn't know what it should mean, but it burst.

"Okay, so what does all this mean?"

Ford looked to Noah, and I followed his gaze.

"What, because my parents happen to be a triad, I have to be the expert on triads?" Noah said with a laugh.

I leaned back into Ford as we stared at Noah, who shrugged.

"Fine, the biggest thing that I know about relationships from my parents is that you have to be open and communicate. You have to trust the other two in the relationship, and you have to speak up. And there has to be a relationship beyond just the three people. If that makes sense."

"As in, Noah and I have a relationship, and Greer?" Ford whispered. "You and I would be together, and then you and Noah would be together if that's what you want."

My heart raced, my lips went dry, and my tongue darted out to lick them.

Noah groaned audibly as Ford chuckled low in my ear. "Okay, we've got the heat there. What do you say?"

"I say yes," Noah blurted. "I say we talk about it, and we be fucking careful, but I say yes."

There was something else in his gaze, something I was missing. Maybe this was stupid, but I didn't want it to end.

"Okay, let's try this out. But if it doesn't work, we walk away still as friends. You two have to remain friends. I will not be the woman that breaks up the band."

"We all know she didn't break up that band," Ford said into my ear, his breath warm against my skin. I shivered and, without thinking, I turned and brushed my lips against his. He groaned, sliding his hands in my hair, as he slowly explored my mouth.

He was so warm, so hot, and I pressed my thighs together, trying to think as he kissed me. When he finally backed away, Noah's hand slid along the back of my neck. I turned and parted my lips as he kissed me.

Noah was slightly rougher, his lips just a bit fuller. He kissed like he was a starving man and I was his salvation. I slid my hand up his chest, my fingernails digging in, and he groaned into me.

I moved back, trying to catch my breath. My nipples ached, two hard little points against my bra. I knew I was wet, and I pressed my thighs together, trying not to come just from kisses alone.

Both men followed the motion with their eyes, and then, as if in sync, they adjusted themselves, their hard cocks pressing against their jeans.

"Wow," I whispered, and Noah grinned.

"One more thing," Noah said casually, then he leaned over me, and crushed his mouth to Ford's. I was pressed between them, could feel the hard ridges of their erections as they bracketed me on the couch. They kissed harder, rougher, and my hands were on both of them.

And when they parted, I sucked in a deep breath.

"Okay, that was the hottest thing I've ever seen."

"You haven't seen anything yet," Ford purred into my ear.

Then Noah's phone buzzed and he cursed.

"It's that damn client," Noah growled.

Ford's phone buzzed as well, and he pulled up the screen. "Looks like they need us both. Fuck," Ford growled.

"It's okay," I said, fanning myself. "I think having a threesome on this couch after our first date might have been too much for me anyway," I lied, though I wasn't really sure it was a lie.

They gave me knowing looks.

"Okay, I need a quick cold shower, then I'll be out," Ford said with a shake of his head. "You okay with us leaving you alone tonight?"

"As much as it would be amazing to continue this, this was a lot, so yes, let's put a pause on what was going to happen on this couch. I'm good. I promise."

They each kissed me again before going into work. I had never been more grateful for a text.

Because I wanted them, and I knew they wanted me. But I was in over my head, and I needed a moment.

Even if I knew exactly what would happen next.

Chapter 9
FORD

My phone buzzed beside me on my desk, and I answered with a smile. "Can't get enough of me?" I asked, knowing my brother Aston on the other end would just roll his eyes at me. I could practically see it, honestly.

"Somebody's full of himself," my big brother said with a deep laugh.

Aston was the eldest of us. Technically, I was the baby of the family, but I didn't like to think about it like that. I bullied my brothers into submission just like they did to me. It didn't matter that I was nearly a decade younger than Aston, he and I were friends. And we gave each other shit. That's what big brothers and little brothers did for each other.

"Is this about dinner?" I asked. We didn't get to all

meet every week, but we tried to have regular Cage family dinners. Much like Noah's family, we had a set time every week where as many of us as possible tried to meet up. It didn't always work out, but when we lost our mother a few years ago, we wanted to make sure that we kept up with everything that she taught us. To be good kids, and to care about each other. And, in my brothers' eyes, how to grow even stronger and more powerful so we could beat the Montgomerys.

My lips twitched, thinking about what they would say when they realized that Noah was no longer just my best friend and roommate. Not that I knew what label to put on us because we had only been on one date, and then spent a few hours making out the following day. I didn't really feel like we knew what we were doing, but I was trying. At least a little.

"Actually, I'm calling about a meeting."

I nodded, my head lifting at the sound of Jennifer's laugh. She was working with Gus over at her desk, both of them having just returned from a job.

She'd pulled her head back, and I could see the bruise on her chin. Some guy had tried to get a little too close to our client, and Jennifer had put her body on the line. That had been three days ago, and the bruise was still there. The fact that I'd had to practically pull Gus off the entire detail because he had lost his mind concerned me.

I didn't know what was going on between the two of them but, if someone had done that to Noah, I wasn't sure I wouldn't act the same. There was probably a reason you shouldn't get involved with people at work, but I wasn't going to think about that, especially not with my brother on the other line who always knew the tones in my voice.

"Okay, a work meeting, or dinner meeting?"

"Honestly, they are the same thing. You run our security teams over here after all."

I pushed the thoughts of inter-workplace relationships out of my mind and nodded even though my brother couldn't see me. "And we appreciate your business, considering I know you could hire your own."

"You could be part of Cage Enterprises."

I rolled my eyes at the familiar refrain. Cage Enterprises was large enough that they had their own security teams. My brothers were real estate developers, but not the crazy mustache-twirling kinds who evaded taxes and tried to blow up the world. They were environmentally conscious ones who did their best to actually use the land and resources that were available to them. They worked with the Montgomerys to make sure that whatever they developed was used correctly and responsibly. If my brother could, he would go hug a tree before building a park around it that was so beautiful, people wept.

But that was my brother, an enigma.

The security teams that protected the main building where the Cage Enterprises was located, as well as all of their sites, were run by us. We trained them, and ensured they knew what they were doing. Our security team and Cage Enterprises worked together to hire them, but we were in charge of keeping everyone on their toes.

It really would've been easier if they hired their own and kept everything in-house. But for my brother, having me be part of the company was keeping it in-house.

However, he couldn't help but get those little licks in.

"You could be part of Cage Enterprises," he repeated.

"I like Montgomery Security." It didn't matter that I wasn't a Montgomery, it mattered that I loved what I was doing, and the people I did it with.

"Interesting, there's something different in your voice."

I held back a curse because I knew this would happen. Aston was way too good at this. He should have been on my side of the job. Of course, then that meant I would have to orchestrate an entire company and figure out what I was doing with a billion dollars or some shit like that. So not my thing.

"Okay, now that you're trying to figure out little tics in my voice, I know this phone call's ended. Let's set up that meeting, and we'll go through what you need. I'll send Daisy over too."

"You do that," Aston practically purred, and I narrowed my eyes.

"Hands off Daisy."

"Of course. I wouldn't dare hit on sweet Daisy."

"Okay, I don't want to know, do I?"

"There's nothing to know. She's formidable. She could kick my ass."

"Damn straight Daisy could," I said, as Daisy walked in the room right as I said her name. She narrowed her eyes at me, and I wanted to hide underneath my desk.

"Okay, got to go," I said after we confirmed our time, and I set my phone down.

"Why did you say my name? What evil things are you planning?" Daisy asked as she made her way to her desk.

"I was just talking to my brother. I was saying I was going to send you over for a meeting, but maybe I won't."

Daisy smiled, her eyes going soft. "Aw, I'll go say hi to Aston. He's really sweet."

Jennifer leaned forward. "Is he the hot one with the short hair on the sides and longer on top, who wears a three-piece suit like he was born in it?"

Gus scowled at her, and she waved him away. Daisy leaned against her desk, her arms folded over her chest. "Oh yes. You see Ford over there? All gruff and a little dirty."

"I'm not dirty," I pouted. Since when did I pout?

"Anyway, his brothers? A whole variety. But Aston? He's beautiful in that suit. There are a couple others who wear suits, and oh my, when they walk towards you it's like you're in Milan in a fashion show and you just want to swoon at their feet. And I don't swoon."

Jennifer leaned forward, ignoring the way that Gus tried to pull her back. "Really. Are they single?" she asked, before looking at me.

"I have no idea. None are married if that helps."

"Really…" Jennifer said again, drawing out the word.

"Don't date my brothers. Things will get complicated if you date my brothers."

"Oh, yes, coming from you of all people, no let's not mix business with pleasure," Daisy said, as everyone stared at me.

I closed my eyes. "Okay, enough of this conversation. I need to get to work."

"We're not going to talk about it?" Gus asked, leaning back in his chair.

"Talk about what?" I asked, ignoring the prickling sensation at my spine as Noah walked in.

"About the fact that I'm pretty sure the date between the three of you went well," Gus drawled.

Noah's gaze shot to mine, and I held up my hands. "I didn't say anything."

"Neither did I," he growled.

"Excuse me, you know what we do for a living, right?" Daisy asked, raising a brow.

"You were spying on us?" I asked, eyes wide.

"It's not spying if you're making out with each other on camera on our damn property."

I could feel the tips of my ears blush, but Noah scowled.

"Stop spying."

"Again, it's not spying if you're the ones that set up the fucking cameras." Daisy shook her head, but it was Jennifer who laughed.

"Seriously, the best show. And as for how we knew about the date? You guys were talking about it at work when you were making plans. It's not my fault if I happened to be walking by the open door. You guys really should close doors."

I closed my eyes at that familiar refrain, grateful they didn't know exactly what had happened the last time we hadn't closed the door. Dear God, we were really not good at this.

"Don't give Greer shit about this," Noah ordered, pointing at all of them.

Gus raised his hands in surrender. "I would never. Hell, Greer is now my favorite person for taking on the two of you." He cringed, shook his head. "I meant emotionally, not whatever dirty way all of your minds went. Because damn, you guys are intimidating as it is and you're just my bosses. I can't imagine actually going on a date with you."

"That's oddly introspective of you," Jennifer said, her voice holding back laughter. "Of course, now we want to know how the date went."

"We need to get back to business," Noah snarled before he stomped to his desk.

I shook my head, my heart racing for some reason. Oh, I knew the reason, but I wasn't going to deal with it. "Enough mixing our personal lives with work. We need to actually focus."

"You really should have thought of that before you started a company with the Montgomerys and how many of their cousins? Sorry, that doesn't work for me," Jennifer said with a laugh.

"Stop putting logic into this. You're the one who came into this business after we had already formed it. You knew what you were getting into."

"Oh honey, nobody knows what they're getting into with the Montgomerys." She winked as she said it, and Gus once again scowled at her. "But the Cages? I'd like to get to know them."

Daisy just beamed. "We'll talk."

"I don't want to know," I said, rubbing my temples. "I really don't want to know."

WHEN WE FINALLY FINISHED UP WORK AND meetings for the day, I jumped into Noah's SUV and sighed.

"What the hell are we doing?" I asked Noah as he drove us home. We had carpooled that day because Noah was the only one with offsite meetings.

"We're fucking things up, but at least we're doing okay about it," he said with the laugh.

"You know, probably, but whatever. I'm trying not to fuck things up."

"I know. Same here." And then Noah did something that startled me, and yet soothed something inside me. He reached over and gripped my hand, tangling his fingers with mine.

"I'm going to try to be better. And not so growly." He paused, waiting for my laugh to finish. "Okay, apparently, I'm always growly, but so are you. However, I'm going to try not to run away when things get hard. And no, I'm not just talking about my dick."

I laughed so hard, tears slid down my cheeks, but I didn't let go of his hand.

"We're doing this. We're trying."

"I guess so. But I don't want to lose you, Noah."

"I don't want to lose you, Ford. I don't know what I'd do if I did."

We were silent as we pulled into the driveway, our

fingers still tangled. "We're talking. And you're holding my hand. I guess that's something."

Noah met my gaze, then leaned forward, brushing his lips against mine.

"You're my best friend, Ford. And Greer in there? I really like her. Just like I really like you. So we're complicated, but we're figuring it out. At least, I hope."

I met those blue eyes of his that always made me think things I shouldn't. "Let's go inside and say hello to our girl."

Noah's smile was slow, his gaze dark. "I like the sound of that. Our girl."

"Damn straight."

We got out of the car and made our way inside, and I smiled when I heard music blaring, saw Horatio sleeping on the couch, and Greer dancing in the kitchen. She was cooking up something, her ass moving side to side as she swayed, and I couldn't stop looking at it. It was so wide and yet soft and cuddly and firm all at once. Maybe I was losing my mind, because I just wanted to go down on my knees and press my face against her ass. Yes, there was something wrong with me.

I met Noah's gaze, and as we set down our things, as quietly as possible, he nodded.

Oh, this was going to be fun.

We tiptoed towards her softly, and when she whirled

she dropped the empty metal bowl in her hands and screamed.

I cursed, and ran to her, gripping her hips.

"I'm sorry. We wanted to surprise you, but I realize now that it probably just scared the fuck out of you."

"I knew you guys were coming home soon, hence why I was chopping up a salad, but oh my God. Heart attack." She put her hands between her ample breasts and tried to catch her breath. "Okay. Now that I'm trying to breathe again, hi."

My hands were still on her hips, and I leaned down and brushed my lips against hers.

"Hello," I whispered.

Then Noah was there, sliding in behind her as he slid his hands up her sides, to cup her breasts.

Her eyes widened, but she leaned back against him.

"Well, hello stranger," she said with a laugh as she tilted her head up. Noah took her lips a little harder, and she moaned, rocking against both of us. And just like that, my dick hardened and pressed against her stomach.

"I could get used to this," I said with a laugh.

"Well, I was going to turn on this stove and start boiling water, but I think it's hot enough in here that I don't need to."

Noah leaned forward and nipped her chin. "I can't stop thinking about you," he growled.

"Seriously, do you know how hard it is to work with a

hard-on because all I can do is think about you bent over this morning when you were trying to reach something?" I asked.

She moaned, Noah's hands still on her breasts, her body arching toward me and I could feel the heat of her between her legs against my thigh.

"Oh, thank God, because all I could do today was think about the two of you, and I wanted to go over to your work just to say hello, and then I realized we'd probably make out or end up fucking in one of the offices, and I don't know how many security cameras you guys have."

I thought about what the others had said, about how they had seen Noah and me kissing on the cameras.

"Yeah, there may be too many cameras around for something like that."

She raised a brow. "What did the cameras catch before?"

"Why don't we show you?" Noah asked before he leaned forward and took my lips. I groaned, pressing into Greer as she wrapped her hands around my waist, pulling me impossibly closer.

"That is so fucking hot," she whispered.

I pulled away from Noah and looked down at her. "Anything we need to put in the fridge? Anything going to spoil?"

Her eyes widened, and she shook her head. "I just

started, actually."

"So why don't we finish," I whispered, sliding my hand between her legs over her jeans. She was hot. So hot, and when she rocked her hips into my hand, I groaned.

"Let's get you in the bedroom."

Horatio meowed behind us, and Greer winced. "Oh yes. Let's not scar the cat."

"But I guess I will play with this pussy," I teased, cupping her again.

She rolled her eyes, even as she groaned as I ground the palm of my hand against her.

"That was a horrible joke."

"It's okay, we'll make him apologize on his knees," Noah teased, winking at me.

This felt right. So damn right. And I knew if I thought about it too hard it would all break, so I wasn't going to think about it.

It might be a mistake, but I didn't care.

The three of us made our way back to my bedroom, though I wasn't sure it was even a conscious thought where we ended up. It didn't matter, we each had a bed, and in the end, we would end up tangled together.

"Tell us what you're up for?" I asked, as we stood at the edge of the bed, our hands roaming over each other. Greer bit her lip, and I leaned forward, kissing the mark she made.

Her eyes rolled back, and she leaned against Noah, who had his hands on her breasts, still playing with her nipples over her shirt.

"I want you both inside of me. I, well, I've used toys before, so I'm okay with anal," she said, her face blushing so hard that I couldn't help but lean down and kiss the heat.

"Dear God, I think I'm going to blow right here," Noah said with a laugh.

I shook my head and gripped her hips a little tighter. "Okay. That sounds like a treat. And you're okay with Noah and me touching?" I asked.

Noah nodded, letting me lead. Which wasn't like him, usually he was the one who led, but I understood with this, because I was able to speak in this moment, I would. We needed to know exactly what Greer wanted, what she could handle. Because Noah and I wanted everything. But that might be a little too much for our first time.

"I've already seen the two of you fuck, and it was the hottest thing I've ever seen in my life. So please touch. *Please.*"

I leaned down and kissed her again, then kissed Noah as well. "Let's see where this leads us, but I'd like right now to be all about you. It is our first time after all."

Noah nodded. "Oh yes, you can watch me take Ford later."

"Excuse me, I do believe it's my turn," I teased.

"Oh my God, do guys take turns? Okay, I'm just going to come right here, you just let me be. I'll let you know when I'm done."

I nipped at her lip, and then we were falling on the bed, laughing, as our hands roamed.

I stripped off my shirt, as did Noah, then I slowly did the same for Greer. Her breasts were full, practically falling out of her bra, and I tugged one lacy cup down, her cherry pink nipple firm and tight.

"You're so fucking sexy. I love your breasts. They overfill my hand, and I just want to lick and suck them."

"I always feel that they're too big. It's hard to even jog because I bounce around too much, even with a tight sports bra."

"Okay, so that's an image that I'm going to take with me to the spank bank," Noah teased.

"Who says spank bank anymore?" I said with a laugh.

"I don't know, I'm just trying not to come right now, so I'm making up jokes."

"Oh, I'm trying not to come right now as well, because I've never had more than one orgasm at a time, and I'm not sure I can take more than that."

I met Noah's gaze, then we both grinned and Greer let out a groan.

"Please don't take that as a challenge. Seriously, I'll be a wet noodle."

"Oh, you'll be wet. And fuck yes we're taking that as a challenge." I laughed and bent down to lick her nipples.

"Oh, you're going to come more than once. And we're going to fuck that pretty pussy of yours, that mouth, those breasts, and your ass. What do you say about that?" Noah asked.

"Anything, it's all yours, as long as you guys come as well."

"Oh, don't worry. We will," I teased. "However, I need to find our condoms."

"I'm on birth control, but yes, I'd like condoms if that's okay."

"Damn straight. We're always going to keep you safe," I said, my voice solemn, and then there was no more talking for a while. We touched, stripping each other, taking our time. I didn't know how we were even able to take our time, considering I knew all three of us wanted to get down to business, go hard and fast, but this seemed important, just to take our time and explore.

Because honestly, this could all go away in a moment. I refused to let it, I refused to lose it.

Noah found himself leaning back against the headboard, as he slid his hands through Greer's hair. She knelt in front of him, slowly sucking his cock up and down, using his free hand to play with her nipples. I knelt behind her, spreading her cheeks, as I leaned down and finally had a sweet taste. She rocked against Noah's cock as I licked and sucked at her sweet pussy, playing with her clit.

"You're so fucking soft, so wet," I teased, as I used her wetness to slide back and ease my finger a little deeper.

She groaned as I slid the butt plug in, loving the way that she knew exactly what to do.

"Just to prepare you, because our cocks are slightly bigger than this."

"Such a tease," she said with a groan, before she went back to sucking Noah's cock. I went back to licking and sucking her pussy, until she was shaking in front of me, and I finally speared her with two fingers. She came, her pussy clamping around my fingers as she rocked into me.

"That's one," I teased.

"Oh my God!" she called out, but we weren't even close to being done yet.

We moved positions, so Noah was behind her and I was under her, taking her breasts in my mouth as Noah pumped me, all three of us sliding into one another. We changed again, this time Greer sitting on my lap, my condom-clad cock pressed against her, but not inside. We were taking our time, although the wait was excruciating. Noah was behind her, playing with her nipples, before reaching down and playing with the plug.

"So full, and you guys aren't even inside me yet."

"Patience," I whispered, biting her lip.

"Please, no more patience."

Noah laughed, and then he slid the butt plug out.

We hadn't decided who would go first, who would go where, but it didn't matter. Because I was on my back, she was finally sliding over me. Her pussy was so tight, so wet, that it took a moment, but it felt like coming home.

Her hands shook, and when Noah reached around and pressed his fingers along her clit, she came again.

She moaned and I smiled, knowing tonight was going to be exhausting for all of us, because we weren't even close to being done.

I slowly moved in and out of her as Noah worked her hole, and then she was bent over me, her breasts pressed against my chest, as Noah slowly began to enter her.

"Are you okay? I can stop," Noah murmured as Greer let out a pained groan.

"No, it feels good. You're not hurting me, I promise."

"You say the word and we'll stop this right now."

"This is what I want. Please. I'm so close."

I reached between us, sliding my hand along her clit

again, and somehow she came. Noah slid deep inside her with one more thrust. And then we were both balls deep, and Greer was shaking between us, all of us sweat slick.

"I can't, there's no, no," and Greer couldn't say anything else, so Noah and I continued to move. When Noah leaned over her to take my lips, and then tilted Greer's head to take hers, I knew that this was it. This was one night of perfection.

We moved slowly, then a bit harder, and it didn't matter.

Because she was coming again, her body going limp, and I knew she was spent. I gripped her hips, met her gaze and then Noah's as I came, Noah following right along.

The orgasm tightened my balls, and my entire body bowed, feeling as if I had been struck by lightning.

I couldn't breathe, I couldn't do anything but hold them.

Noah finally moved away and brought wet towels to clean us. I moved her sweat slick hair back from her face, as she blinked lazy eyes down at me.

"Are you okay?"

"I think I'm better than okay, but once I wake up from this dream which is much better than any dream that I've ever had with the two of you guys before, I'll let you know."

Noah gave a rough chuckle before he kissed her shoulder, then leaned over to kiss me.

"Well, I guess that's more than one," he said, so cocky I had to roll my eyes.

"You guys win. Of course, I think I'm the one who won here."

I gripped her hip as I pulled the blanket over us, cuddling in with the two of them.

"Oh, I think we all win."

"Well, I am one lucky lady. I think I should say thank you."

Her voice was sleep-slurred, and I kissed her temple before wrapping my arm around them both.

"I want to keep her," Noah whispered, surprising me. And from the look on his face, he immediately regretted the words. Not for Greer, but for him. Greer slept in our arms, and I nodded.

He had wanted to run away, to push Greer and me together because he hadn't thought this would work. I nodded and pulled him closer, because I knew he meant the words, and I wanted to believe that this could happen.

That this was it.

And maybe it could be.

Maybe, just maybe, I could get everything that I ever wanted.

Finally.

Chapter 10
NOAH

"WHAT'S WRONG?" I ASKED AS FORD STOMPED BACK into the office, phone in his hand and a glare on his face. I wanted to reach out and cup his chin, force him to look at me, but we were at work. And though we were blending everything else in our lives, we decided it would be easier if we didn't make out at work, because we were the bosses, and we didn't need to screw everything up in every aspect of our lives.

"I swear to God, I'm going to scream if I have to deal with that woman one more time."

I raised a brow, grateful that we didn't have any clients in the building. But it wasn't like Ford to blurt things without thinking.

"Was it her again? I didn't know you have her on the docket."

"I don't. Daisy helped her yesterday, and apparently she wasn't happy. She somehow got my phone number and won't stop texting me."

Alarmed, I sat up straighter. "What the hell? We're unlisted for a reason."

"Yeah well, it's my personal number, and you know we use our numbers for every fucking thing to log in. I guess I'm listed somewhere, and she found me."

I cursed and held out my hand for his phone. "Let me see."

"You want to see her texting me and raging that I'm not helping her?"

"Yes, and then you're going to tell Daisy about it, we're going to stop working for Jocelyn Price."

Ford ran a hand over his face and slid over the phone. "I hate this. I don't know why she suddenly either has it in for me or decided that we meant something more to each other than her being a client that I set up security for. I don't want her to feel unsafe, but dammit, it's getting weird."

I rubbed my temple as Gus walked in, box in hand.

"What's that?" I asked, exhausted already. It was a long day, and I still needed to go work with my clients after they had postponed our appointment four times.

"Just some of the equipment that we pulled from the last appointment. It's bugging me, and I want to figure out if I can fix it."

Gus was a whizz with technology, and I nodded. "Sounds good. Do you need help?"

"You have an appointment to go to, don't you?" Ford asked as he held out his hand for his phone. I had already copied everything over, scowling at the texts demanding that Ford help her in every way possible.

No, we would not be working with Jocelyn Price anymore. And I would make sure that either I or Daisy would handle it. I knew Kane and Kingston would as well, but since I was here, and Daisy had been the one to work with her last, it would be one of us.

Nobody hurt Ford. He was mine, if only for the moment, so I wasn't going to let anyone hurt him.

"You're working with Henderson again today?" Ford asked, and I sighed.

"How do you know?"

"Because you get this little pulse at your temple whenever you think of him." Ford reached out and brushed his finger along my temple. I froze, my gaze going to Gus, who just smiled quietly and went back to his work.

When I scowled at Ford, my best friend and lover shrugged, as if he hadn't just touched me at work when we were trying not to do that.

"Anyway, I'm going to work on a few things and then I need to head up to my brothers'. You sure you don't want to go?" Ford asked and I shook my head. I liked dinner with the Cages. It was very much like dinner with my family. Loud, boisterous, with some infighting, but mostly just teasing and lots of good food.

I had been there countless times before, just like Ford ate often with my family, but now things were different.

We were doing our best not to put labels on anything, because if we did that, I knew they would shatter. And I was waiting for Ford to realize we were better off as friends, and for Greer and Ford to realize that they clicked better with just each other. After all, I had grown up in a poly household. I knew things weren't easy. My parents loved each other, got along, and when they fought it wasn't something life-changing, it was something they just needed to discuss. But the outside world didn't always agree. There had been protests at one of my schools when I was a kid, something I barely remembered because my parents had sheltered me from it. There had been a time on a vacation where my mother had been threatened and nearly attacked. There had been slurs and even local governments trying to make laws because certain people on their councils hadn't agreed with my parents' so-called lifestyle. So my aunt and uncle had joined the council themselves, all to protect my parents and our family.

While the sex and the heat and the emotions between us could last, I knew that the real world wasn't always easy. So as long as I didn't screw up my friendship with both of them, I could enjoy this moment, even though my blurted-out instinct of wanting to keep her wasn't going to come to fruition.

"What's going on in your head?" Ford asked as he leaned against my desk, his voice low.

I shook my head, pushing all thoughts of that out of my mind. I had to live in the moment and prepare for the worst. That was my job after all. "Nothing. I'll finish a couple of traces when I get home, but dinner? I have so much shit to do, and I'll probably still be at the Henderson house when you finish. Say hi to the family." I paused, frowning. "You're bringing Greer?"

Ford's brows rose. "I don't think Greer is ready for a family dinner. And then we'd have to flip coins on which family dinner it would be first. Because you know they'll fight over it. Playfully, but they'll do it."

I snorted. "You outnumber my family. At least in terms of my immediate family."

After all, I had two sisters and a brother, but if you added all of the cousins, I had at least twenty. Maybe fifty if I really did the math with the extended family. But Ford had six brothers.

"We'll flip a coin when the time comes for something like that. But you've been to countless dinners at my family's house."

I was aware Gus was listening, because it wasn't like we were being quiet, but I still lowered my voice. "And it would be different now, wouldn't it? I don't know. Maybe I'm just overthinking."

"Well, that makes sense. You think harder than anyone."

"Amen." We both scowled at Gus, who just shrugged, equipment all over his desk as he studied it. "What? It's not like you guys were in a secret room. You're having an important conversation right in front of me. Either way, I hope you guys figure it out. It's about fucking time."

"Gus," Ford began, and I just laughed.

"If you're going to ask questions about us, I'm going to ask questions about a certain somebody that you work with."

As Ford held back laughter, Gus shut his mouth, his eyes going wide before he scowled. Then the other man went back to work without another word, and I figured we were even.

"And on that note, I'm taking my phone and going back to work. Then I'm going to dinner. Good luck with the Henderson house."

I just shook my head, knowing it was going to take more than luck. I finished up my work and shot off a quick text to Daisy so she knew what we needed to do about Ford's client. She sent an eyeroll emoji, then a skeleton, and I just shook my head, knowing that she wanted to kick ass as much as I did. Nobody hurt Ford, even though I knew I might.

Instead, I made my way to the client's house. Nolan Henderson stood on the front porch, arms folded over his wide chest. The man was former special ops, and could probably break me with a single pinky, and that was saying something, since I worked out every day and was trained in multiple fighting styles. But Nolan was trained to kill. At least, that's what the guys had said when they had seen him, and though we had been joking, I wasn't sure we were off the mark.

I pulled in front of the single-story home with gray shutters, a two-car garage, and bars over the windows. We hadn't added them, and I had a feeling the HOA wasn't pleased with them. But Nolan Henderson got what he wanted when it came to keeping his place secure —even if it made no sense.

"You're late," Nolan said from the porch, and I looked down at my phone. I was six minutes early, but I didn't say anything. Nolan was the type of guy who thought that being fifteen minutes early was on time and being on time was late. And while I agreed with him, if I had shown up fifteen minutes early like I had the first time, Nolan would've berated me for being early enough to waste time and block his driveway. Which I hadn't done, but the guy loved finding things to pick at.

I nodded and pointed towards the camera that was malfunctioning.

"I'll get to work," I said, my voice low, not bothering

to even introduce myself again or say hello. The other man wouldn't appreciate it.

"I'll be watching you. I want to make sure it's done right this time."

"No problem. Would you like me to explain what I'm doing?"

"I know what you're doing. I'm not an idiot. I've seen more and done more than you could ever dream of, boy."

I sighed internally because if I did it audibly, I'd have to deal with the man's attitude. Then I got to work, ignoring the way Mr. Henderson continued to try to explain how to do my job. The thing was, the other man was wrong. He didn't know what he was doing, and the reason that the thing was malfunctioning wasn't our fault. Someone had clearly fucked with it. And I had a feeling if I looked at the feed, it would be Nolan himself. He thought he knew best and wanted to fix something he thought was broken. I didn't say anything though, because I would need proof in order to figure out what to do about him as a client, so I just got to work and listened to the man berate me.

"There's another few things I need you to look at. Come."

"On it," I said.

"I'm your elder, you should call me sir."

"Mr. Henderson, we both know that I'm not doing that."

He glared at me and I could have kicked myself.

"I'm sorry. That was rude."

"Damn straight it was." He mumbled things that I didn't want to hear, and it made me wonder why he'd even hired our company. There were other companies that would serve his needs just as well that would have the same opinions he did. I glanced through a window and saw a hate sign in bright colors and kicked myself. Shit. If this guy found out that the people keeping him secure were mostly queer and thought all people deserved equal rights, things would hit the fan.

If I had my way, this would be our last visit here. I'd ask the crew, but I had a feeling they'd agree. We didn't serve hate.

We turned the corner and Nolan pointed up at the side of the house. "You missed this. How many other things are you missing?"

I frowned at the place where a camera could have been, but Henderson had decided he didn't want one there. I just took notes and explained the next step of installation for the project.

"If you'd like that, we can work that for you."

"Damn straight. I want the best." He paused. "I heard about what happened in your building. You missed that, too, didn't you? Some serial killer or something just living right next to you. I don't know why I keep hiring you, but the wife liked that you hire women. Though I don't know why you would." He continued to rant sexist and rude drivel, but all I could do was hear my heartbeat in my ears.

Because he was talking about the man I had missed. The man who had hurt Raven, and so many others. He wasn't a serial killer, had never killed anyone. But he hurt them. And it could have been worse. But there was no paper trail, there had been no sign of what that man was.

But there must have been. I hadn't dug deep enough. That had to be the case.

I hadn't protected my family enough.

I swallowed hard and let the man berate me, I deserved it for that. And then I finished installing and made sure he knew the bill was coming. The man growled, and I had a feeling we'd be losing another client. We needed the money, needed the clients, but we didn't need to deal with this bullshit every day.

Annoyed, I thought maybe I should have gone with Ford to his family's house, get some dinner, and be with people who actually liked me. But I wasn't in the mood.

I was tired and pissed off.

I parked in the garage next to Greer's car and was relieved she was there. At least, grateful because I liked being near her, but she didn't need to see this mood. So when I walked inside to the scent of some form of curry, I stopped in my tracks.

"You're cooking?"

She smiled over at me and nodded toward the pot on the stove. "Yes, I'm trying a new recipe but I'm realizing the whole house is going to smell like curry for like the next few days. So I opened up all the windows, and now Horatio is in the back window, meowing at a bird." She rolled her eyes, and a little bit of the tension from the day left my shoulders.

It was amazing that she could do that. Just one look, a little laugh, and I could breathe again. I couldn't rely on that. I knew things would change.

"Smells damn good."

"Well thank you. Are you hungry?"

"I wasn't, but now I am." My voice got a little deeper when I said that.

"I meant for food."

"Honestly I did too."

"Okay good. Because I really want to try this. I know Ford's with his brothers, but the leftovers will still be good."

"I didn't know you cooked like this," I said as I set my things down on the kitchen island.

"I don't always, Raven's the better cook. But I like to try new things. And since I got my favorite wok out of storage, I figured now was a good time to test a new recipe."

Not able to help it, I leaned forward and brushed the hair back from her face that had fallen out of her ponytail. And then I kissed her softly. She opened for me, sighing into my mouth.

"Hello."

"I was going to say welcome home, but that felt a little too domestic. And now I realize that I'm sitting here making food, so maybe this is domestic. But after all, we're roommates—who occasionally get to kiss."

"Occasionally," I said, kissing her again. "I'm glad you have some of your things here. That you're settling in."

"It's a little weird but I'm getting used to it. Although I'm realizing there're things that I do need, so I'm constantly adding to my list of things to buy once the insurance check comes in."

There was a look of worry on her face, and I knew it was because we were waiting to see if it was truly arson, or an accident. Because we didn't know who would have done it. It didn't make any sense, and we were in limbo while we waited.

"Anything you need for the house that's shareable, let us know. We've got it."

"No, you don't need to pay for everything for me.

The fact that you're even letting me live here is amazing."

"And you don't need to worry about things that the house needs, because if you think the house needs it, then Ford and I need it too."

"Oh really? That's how easy it is?"

"It can be."

"Hmm," she said, then studied my face and turned off the stove. "What's going on? You have little lines at the sides of your eyes."

I sighed and shook my head. "Do I need to go get Botox or something? Ford and you both mentioned that today," I said laughing, rubbing my temples.

"They're not fine lines, it's just stress. Are you okay?"

I shrugged, and then figured it was good to share part of my day. That's what friends did, didn't they?

"It's just been a long day." I explained about the Henderson and Price accounts, and the fact that we were dealing with customer service that really didn't feel like any service.

"What the hell? Do you *have* to work with them? Or can you just pick better clients?"

"Well, annoying clients need security too. However, we are probably going to drop both of them. We need clients of course, but we do have good word-of-mouth with our good clients, and with Ford's family wanting more and more of our expertise on their jobs, and the

Montgomery Construction arm needing more security as well, we sort of have a waiting list."

"You see? You don't need the stress of these then. You've got this."

She put her hand on my chest, her smile bright, and I leaned down and took her lips with mine again.

"I like this."

She smiled up at me, tilting her head. "You like what? The taste of curry? Because I've been sampling all day."

I snorted, before I took her lips again. "That is a plus. But I like coming home and talking to you. I get to do that with Ford, but we also work together so he usually knows what I'm stressed about. I just like doing both."

She wrapped her arms around my waist and hugged me tight. I held her close to me.

"I like you being here too. It's weird though, how easy this sometimes feels even though I know it's not easy. However, I'm glad that you're home and ready to eat."

I smiled then, and her eyes widened. "Noah."

"You think the dinner will be okay on the stove for just a little bit longer?"

"It's just the lids on the pots, and the heat's off, so it should be fine. What do you have in mind?"

In answer, I gripped her hips and lifted her. She let

out a little squeak and wrapped her arms around my neck, and then wrapped her legs around my waist.

"Noah."

"Don't worry, I promise I won't be long. I just need an appetizer."

I crushed my mouth to hers as I walked her towards the living room. I set her on the back of the couch and let her legs dangle around my waist.

"I just want a little taste."

I kissed her again, running my hands up and down her body. I cupped her breasts, loving how she rocked into me. I slid her shirt up, then her bra, so I could lick at her breasts and taste and touch. She moaned and gripped the couch so she wouldn't fall over. I was very happy she wore a skirt today, and slowly, oh so slowly, slid the skirt up.

"Noah, the windows are open."

"Nobody can see, but that does mean you're not going to be able to scream my name when you come."

"Oh my God," she mumbled, and I knew she was trying to keep her voice low.

It wasn't going to last for long, the neighbors would probably hear.

But I didn't care.

I knelt before her, and groaned at what was waiting for me.

"Where the fuck are your panties, Greer?"

Greer looked down at me and licked her lips. "Um, I may have been playing with a new toy earlier. Just to see if it worked."

Her clit was swollen, her pussy wet, and I swallowed. "What toy?"

"Um, just a little flower thing. I don't know if I really like it."

She blushed, her entire body pinkening, and I smiled.

"And why is that?"

"Because it's supposed to mimic oral sex, but you and Ford are way better at it. I don't know, a little air blowing on my clit is amazing, and it made my toes curl, but your mouth on my pussy? That makes me fall right off this couch."

"Well then, you'd better hold on," I said, just before I leaned forward and licked her cunt. She groaned loudly, and then put her hand over her mouth, trying to hold back her screams.

I spread her, looking at her cunt, her little hard bud of a clit, before I leaned down to suck and to lick. She was wet, her juices covering my beard. I kept at it, loving the way she rocked against my face. When I pressed my nose against her clit, my tongue spearing her, she wiggled against my face. So I kept eating and sucking and taking my fill. She was so beautiful, the way that she arched in front of me, and I wanted more. When she came, she moaned slowly at first, before it reached a crescendo, and I could hear her press her hand to her mouth, trying to keep her voice quiet.

"Noah. I can't."

I smiled before I pulled her off the couch and flipped her around. She was bent over in front of me, ass up, skirt over her hips.

"I was wondering if I could have an appetizer, because I want your cock in my mouth."

"I don't think I can wait," I growled as I played with her tits, loving the way that they filled my hands.

She was still partially dressed, I was fully dressed—I even still had my shoes on. But I reached into the drawer next to the couch and pulled out a length of condoms.

Greer looked over her shoulder at me, eyes widening when she saw what I held.

"What? We like to be prepared," I said, teasing, before I pulled my cock out and slid the condom on. She groaned at the sight, and then I took her hips, spread her cheeks, and slammed into her. She let out a scream that I knew would echo to the neighbors, and I didn't care. Because my groan followed. Her pussy was tight, wet, and it was all I could do not to pummel into her just then. But then she pressed her ass back into my hips, went on her tiptoes, and started to fuck me.

It was hard and fast and wet and loud, and I loved it. I knew the entire neighborhood could probably hear us, and I would deal with the ramifications later, but I didn't care. All that mattered was Greer, her cunt squeezing me as she came again. I followed her.

I slid my hands around her, bringing her back to my front as I slowly slid in and out of her, letting the orgasm take both of us, holding her close, and kissed her neck.

"Damn, talk about an appetizer."

"You're a menace. How am I supposed to face the neighbors?"

"They'll know you're well taken care of. And don't worry, if anyone says anything to you, you tell me. I'll deal with it."

"Noah, I can deal with it too. I promise, I'm strong."

I kissed her again as I angled her face to me. "I know. Now, let's get to that dinner."

She laughed, her whole body shaking against me, and I let myself live in this moment. Because this felt right, even if it was only temporary.

Chapter 11
GREER

THE SCENTS OF COFFEE AND SUGAR FILLED MY NOSE, and I did a little hip dance as I worked on the next order, the idea of a different mixture for the lattes filling my head. As I handed over their order, this time in a big chunky cup versus a disposable one, I smiled, then went to text myself my idea. I loved this café. Most of the time people were in and out, on their way to work or on errands. But sometimes when they worked on their computers or read a book or just wanted to sit with friends and chat, they would order the for-here mugs and get a little cup and saucer, or a big mug the size of your face, and just enjoy themselves. I loved that we used local artists for the mugs. No two were the same, but I enjoyed it all being eclectic.

"Did we get the next order of mugs?" I asked, my mental conversation reminding me to check.

"Soon. They're working on opening up the gallery and shop next door, so they're a little behind on making our order."

I smiled at that, even though the memory of what had happened hurt.

Because the reason the place was in the middle of construction was because of the attack. Because of that man hurting my best friend.

But now it wasn't going to be a bike shop anymore. The place—which had been too big for him to begin with—was now split into two parts. A designing construction firm and space for the Montgomery Construction arm, as well as a small corner art gallery. And in that art gallery, our sculptor and ceramic artist who loved working with clay was making our mugs.

"Good to know, I'm just making notes."

"Are you supposed to have so much caffeine before your appointment?" Raven asked, raising a brow.

I just laughed, shaking my head. "I'll have you know I had a single cup of coffee this morning and have had only water all day."

One of our regulars gasped as they ordered their drink, and I waved. "I know, I'm shocked too."

"I'm on my second cup, and I'm very lucky that I'm going on the other side of the city today because if I wasn't, I'd keep coming back for more coffee. I love this roast, as well as the scent of that Danish."

"She was laminating pastry all night," I teased, as Raven blushed. My best friend sometimes didn't realize how amazing and talented she was.

I loved her to the bottom of my heart, and I knew that she could go great places with her talent. She could work at a French patisserie or a bakery in New York City and be sought after. She could even be a dessert chef at a Michelin Star restaurant, but here she was, co-owning a franchise with me. We were still new, and I knew that this was our starting point, but also could be our culmination of everything. I was just so damn happy.

"Greer Cassidy?" a man asked, as I looked up to see a man holding a vase of flowers.

I frowned, wondering why those flowers looked familiar.

"That's me," I said. "Can I help you?"

"I have a delivery for you," the man said as he handed over the vase, and I noticed that once again they were primroses. This time purple and pink with a yellow center. The arrangement I had received before had been white primroses. That was so weird, and I would have to tell the guys about this. Or maybe it was from them. But I didn't like primroses. They made me think of funerals, mostly because of a book I had once read.

"Oh, thanks."

"No need to sign. They're for you."

Raven gave me a look and I shrugged. "There's no note. That's weird, right?"

"I think you should tell the guys."

"Yeah. Unless it is from them and then I'm not being appreciative enough. It's weird."

"I don't know. But I think that I'm allergic to them," Raven said as she rubbed her nose.

She immediately went to wash her hands, before I walked outside and set the primroses on one of the outdoor tables. Hopefully they were fine out there, if not I would get rid of them. I just didn't like primroses, and the guys knew that.

"Are you okay?" Raven asked when I walked inside.

I nodded. "Yes. I just don't know who's sending me flowers."

"And you don't think it's one of them?" Raven asked, her voice low.

The world didn't need to know that I was technically sleeping with two men. Maybe dating, but we weren't truly putting labels on anything because that got serious and weird and we didn't need that in our lives.

I shook my head. "I don't think it's them. I mean, they're two doors down, wouldn't they just bring it themselves?"

"Unless they want to be romantic. Sebastian usually

gives me flowers himself, but maybe the guys couldn't because they're on site today."

I snapped my fingers. "You're right. They're on site. They told me that they would be out all day. I don't know why I didn't remember that."

"Maybe because you've been a little busy?" Raven said with a shrug as she went back to her latest cupcake project. They were lavender lemon, with an amazing light meringue icing, and my mouth watered.

"I'll talk to them about it later. And maybe say thank you. Just, I don't really know who else would send me flowers."

"Maybe one of your parents or brothers?"

"My parents are too busy thinking about themselves to send me flowers. And my brothers really aren't guys who send flowers without a note. Or not at all. Anyway, I need to head out."

"Have fun. I'll be over soon to watch."

"Creeper," I said with a tease as I went to grab my things.

"Seriously, I'll be over in twenty minutes, the rest of the team has it. I can't wait to see."

I smiled nervously, kissed the top of my best friend's head, and then headed over to Montgomery Ink Legacy.

I'd had this appointment for months, long before the fire and everything changed. I'd almost canceled it, my life in flux, but I wanted this. It was time.

Things were changing, I was changing, but I wanted something just for me.

Of course, that made me think of Noah and Ford. Because they were mine if just for the moment. It felt nice to be with them. To wake up beside one or both of them. It was even nice to wake up by myself, knowing that they were just a room or two away. We were going with the flow, figuring things out. It was fun. But I knew it wasn't forever. Things like this didn't last forever. But I felt special with them, they made sure of it.

I had never felt that way in any of my past relationships. I knew Matt had tried, but my heart hadn't been in it, and he hadn't been for me.

But Noah and Ford? They made me feel special.

But they were in love with each other, even if they didn't see it yet. So I was grateful for this time. Grateful for this moment with them, and the fact that while my life was in limbo, I had time to breathe with them.

I still had my business, I still had a future I was trying to find, but I had this break.

This fun.

And I was going to enjoy it.

I walked into the shop, and Leif Montgomery smiled up at me. "I was afraid you were going to cancel and I was going to have to pull you through the side door. Which, why didn't you come through it?"

Leif Montgomery was one of Noah's many cousins, and beautiful and rugged like the rest of them. He was older than Noah by around a decade, and married with two kids. He also owned the shop with his friends and family just like Noah owned his. I knew that the Legacy part of the name actually was a legacy. His father was a tattoo artist, and worked with Noah's mother who also owned Montgomery Ink in downtown Denver. It was all in the family, and I could have had my pick of any Montgomery to do my tattoo. But Sebastian would be doing mine, because Raven's love would not let anyone else touch my skin. Of course, if and when I met Maya Montgomery, Noah's mother, that might all change. I had met her in passing, but not since being with her son. And that wasn't something I wanted to think about.

At least not when I was already nervous.

"I'm sorry, and I went through the outside because I needed a little bit of fresh air before doing such a big thing."

"You're going to do great. Though I am a little jealous it's not my turn."

"Always just so jealous," Sebastian said as he came out from the back, notebook in hand.

Of all the people in the shop, Sebastian was the most inked up and pierced. He might be younger, but he had taken the time he had and made art with it. He had been through hell and back, but now he was happy, whole, and father to one of the best little girls I had ever met in my life. The fact that Raven was one day going to be a stepmom shocked me, but not really. Those three clicked, and I reveled in their happiness.

"I'm here, and no need to fight. But we all know that if I went with anyone but Sebastian, Raven would beat us all."

Leif nodded. "That is true." He looked over my shoulder. "I thought she'd be with you."

"My girl just texted and said she'd be over soon," Sebastian said, a sly smile on his face when he said 'my girl.' I loved the two of them and the way they interacted. The fact that Sebastian was smiling more than I had ever seen him before just made everything worth it.

"She's not alone don't worry," Daisy said as she walked through the door, a grin on her face. "I'm not late, am I?"

"I just got here," I said as I hugged Daisy tight. She hugged me right back. "Okay let's get started. I can't wait to see."

"Brooke would be here, but the baby has a cold."

I put my hand over my heart. "I'm sorry, Leif. Are you okay?"

"I'm fine, I took the morning shift, Brooke's taking the afternoon. It's just the sniffles, but with the baby feeling poorly, she decided to stay home."

"You should go," another man said as he walked out from the back. This was Nick, Leif's best friend, and married to Lake Montgomery, yet another cousin.

I only had three brothers, and they were enough, even though I rarely saw them. I couldn't imagine so many other family members.

"I was thinking about it, but I really wanted to see Greer's ink."

"Okay, now I'm nervous," I said with a blush.

"I thought the guys would be here," Sebastian said, raising a pierced brow at me.

"They're on assignment right now, but they might show up for the end," Daisy said, and I blushed even harder.

"Okay, it's just a tiny tattoo. We don't need to freak out."

"But it's virgin skin. I'm excited," Sebastian said as he rubbed his hands together, his gleeful tone making me laugh.

"The way you said that, it's kind of like 'it rubs the lotion on its skin so it doesn't get the hose again.'"

Everybody groaned as Daisy laughed outright.

"No serial killers here. No, really. I can't wait."

"I'm here I'm here, don't start without me," Raven said as she ran inside and smacked a kiss to Sebastian's lips.

"I'll always wait for you."

"Gag," Daisy said with a laugh, as I rolled my eyes.

Leif headed out, waving, as Nick went to work on a client. The client was 6'5", had to be 300 pounds of pure muscle, and kept wincing with every single stroke.

"You've got this. Now, let's go through the sketch again, and then placement."

I wanted ravens. I'd always loved ravens, and then I had found my best friend in Portland with the same name.

I was going to get an unkindness of ravens in a whirlwind down my shoulder and back. We had a whole piece planned, but this was the first part. It would look good on its own until I figured out if I wanted more ink, or if this was going to be it.

"The sketch is great, you have character in each wing."

"That's the goal. Plus, it's not so detailed that it will bleed or anything. So we're good," he said with a nod.

"Okay, place it?"

"Let's do it."

I sat back and talked with the girls as Sebastian worked on the next steps, and when he set the purple trace on my skin, I let out a breath at the temperature drop, and nodded. "It's going to look great. I'll still be able to see one raven on my shoulder in the mirror."

"And you can add on to it, there is no border with this."

"I love it."

"I walk in and see you in a strapless top looking downright sexy," Ford said, and I whirled to see both Noah and Ford there, hands in pockets as they stared at me.

"It's going to look great, man," Noah said, as he looked over at Sebastian.

"Okay, everyone take a seat, because I don't think we need fifteen of us in this space."

"We'll just sit over here," Raven said as she took Daisy's hand and went to one side, and then Ford and Noah were there taking the seats next to me. The room was large enough so it didn't feel overwhelming, but it did feel weird to be sitting in a chair with my back to Sebastian, as the sound of the machine began to whirl.

"Okay. This is fine. I'm totally not going to scream."

Ford reached out and took my hand as Noah leaned against Ford's shoulder, giving me space, but still there.

I didn't miss the way that Raven and Daisy glanced at each other, but I let out a breath, and then Sebastian held my shoulder that wouldn't have ink.

"Are you ready?"

"Yes and no."

Sebastian didn't move. "What's the no?"

"I'm nervous because I don't know how it will feel, but I'm ready."

"You tell me to stop and I will. We've got this. It's going to look beautiful."

I nodded, my gaze on the guys in front of me. I turned to my girlfriends and they smiled, gave me thumbs-up, and then I looked back to meet Ford's and Noah's gazes again.

"So, what're the precautions with this?" Noah asked, even though he had ink of his own. "No hot tubs, right?"

Sebastian nodded, and then he began. At first it was a shock, and I was glad I didn't jump. It felt as if someone was stabbing me with a needle over and over again, but it wasn't sharp. In fact, it sort of felt like a vibration that went to my jaw, and down to my toes, but it almost felt good. Not amazing, but a pain I could deal with. I hummed along it, and Sebastian squeezed my free shoulder.

"No hot tubs, no pools. We're going to put Saniderm over it, and it's breathable and waterproof. Once we're finished we'll figure out exactly how long I want you to keep it on so if you leak plasma it's not a big deal. But tattoo recovery has come a long way over the years."

"You've got this," Noah said.

"I do. It actually feels kind of good."

"Good to know," Ford murmured, as both girls laughed, and Noah just shook his head.

I knew I was blushing, and Sebastian clucked his tongue.

"No flirting. If you flirt and you make Greer blush, and then she starts to shake, I'll fuck up. You don't want me to fuck up."

"Please don't fuck up my tattoo because the guys are being them."

"We'll be good," Noah said.

"For now," Ford added.

The girls burst out laughing, and Sebastian cursed us all out, before continuing.

The tattoo didn't take long, and throughout it all everyone distracted me from the slight pain by talking about the latest movie coming out that we all wanted to go see.

"There's a club opening up downtown. We should try it out."

I turned to Daisy, careful not to move my back or the rest of my body.

"You like clubbing?" I asked.

"Sometimes. We're young, let's have fun."

"You guys are young, I'm an old man," Nick called out.

"Well us young kids can go out and have fun," Raven teased.

"I'll watch the squirts," Nick added, and Sebastian laughed behind me.

"Nora would like that. But yeah, a club sounds good.

Maybe not one that will be so loud it rattles my teeth. But a good drink, some dancing? Why not?"

I looked at the guys in front of me, and Noah nodded. "I know of a few. I think we did security for the one you're talking about, right?" he asked Daisy.

"That's the one. So it'll be safe, we can have fun, and dance our hearts out."

"Sounds good. But maybe in a week or so, so that way you're all healed up," Sebastian said as he shut the machine off. "Okay, let's go through aftercare again, and take a look."

"We're done?" I asked, blinking in surprise.

"We're done. It looks damn good if I do say so myself."

I grinned as I hopped off the chair, and both guys held out their hands, as if waiting for me to fall.

"I'm good. That was fun."

"And you've got another addict," Ford muttered under his breath as he leaned forward and kissed my brow.

Noah did the same and I blushed, knowing that it was mostly just family and friends here, but it was still nice to have them both.

I reminded myself that this was not forever, but I was still special.

I turned my back to the mirror, holding a handheld one so I could see the ink, and I sighed.

"They're beautiful. It looks like they're actually flying."

"You had the idea."

Ford reached out and pushed my hair from my face. "It's beautiful."

"Yeah, damn beautiful," Noah said, as he gripped my hand.

I looked between them, my face heating, and everything else tingling.

"What the hell's going on here?"

I froze at a familiar yet confused voice, and turned to see not one, but all three of my brothers standing there. And from the looks on their faces, they had seen both men touch me, both men kiss me, and they weren't happy.

Not in the slightest.

My pulse raced and I tried to calm myself. I hadn't seen my brothers in over a year. I loved them, and I knew they loved me. But my parents hadn't let me get to know them like I should have.

And here I was, touching two men I was quickly falling for...and lost beyond measure.

"Well? What the fuck is going on?" my eldest brother asked, and as my friends turned towards them, I reached out and gripped both Ford's and Noah's forearms, knowing it was a mistake the moment that my eldest brother saw it.

"You guys, it's fine. Montgomerys and crew? These are my brothers. Brothers, what the hell are you doing here?" I asked, as everyone stiffened, and it felt like the world waited with bated breath for someone to answer.

"We're here because we're worried about our little sister. Seems like we weren't fast enough."

Chapter 12
FORD

I MOVED IN FRONT OF GREER, GLARING AT THE THREE men who were glaring at us.

They all had dark hair, light eyes, and strong jaws. They were clearly brothers, and from what Greer had just said, they were her brothers. Well hell. This wasn't exactly how I had wanted to meet the family, and to be honest, I didn't know much about Greer's past, or her time in Portland. I knew their names, but I didn't know which one was which. I didn't know where they lived, what they did for a living. I knew none of that, because I hadn't had time to get to know her the way I wanted.

That would have to change. We would be fixing shit like actually getting to know each other's pasts as soon as I figured out if I was going to survive this meeting.

"You guys," Greer said as she moved past. The Saniderm was already on her tattoo, and Sebastian stood behind her, arms crossed over his chest as he glared at the three Cassidy brothers.

"Heath. It's fine. I'm fine. Please stop." She reached out and gripped her brother's arm, while Heath, the big behemoth who had spoken, just nodded.

"Greer. You want to introduce us?"

"Do you want to stop acting like a jerk?" Greer asked, and I moved forward, ready to protect Greer if needed, the other brothers seemed to notice the action and adjusted their stances.

"Greer," Heath growled low as he reached for her. Noah and I moved quickly then, standing beside her.

"You're going to want to be careful with her," I said as Noah nodded.

But Greer rolled her eyes, and Raven cursed under her breath before speaking up.

"You guys. We're all on the same side here. We are not having a brawl in a tattoo shop. Boys, you haven't even said hello to me. And it's been over a year."

Sebastian looked over at his woman, his lips twitching into a smile, and I was glad for Raven. Each of the Cassidy brothers relaxed slightly as they turned to Raven.

"Sorry, long flight," the brother who wasn't Heath, but clearly his twin, said.

I hadn't even known Greer had twin brothers. I knew

she had three, and that two were older and one was younger, but it turns out I didn't know enough. I met Noah's gaze, who gave me a tight nod, and I had a feeling that would be changing soon.

But first, introductions.

I cleared my throat. "Sorry about that, long day. I'm Ford. Ford Cage."

Heath looked down at my hand, and then took it slowly. He didn't squeeze, didn't try to show his dominance, instead he just studied my face as if he were searching for answers. I didn't know if I had them to be honest.

"I'm Heath. Greer's older brother. The eldest."

The man's twin rolled his eyes from beside him. "I'm August. And considering he's only about two minutes older than me, he loves lording that over me."

"I'm Noah," my best friend said as he reached out.

"And I'm Luca, the baby." The man rolled his eyes. "At least that's what Greer calls me."

"I'm the youngest too," I said with a laugh. "And I have six older brothers."

"That still makes me shudder to think about," Greer said, as she pressed her arm to mine.

The guys didn't miss the gesture, especially with Noah having his hand on her hip.

Well, this was going to be interesting. I had never been in a poly relationship where I met the family before. Especially a family that seemed to have some issues. I knew that she hadn't grown up with her brothers, and that it was her parents' fault. But I didn't know enough.

"I'm Sebastian, the tattoo artist. So let's be careful with her ink, okay? It's fresh."

"And I'm Daisy, I work with the two lug-heads over here," she said pointing to me and Noah. "Plus, I'm that one's cousin. And that one," she said pointing to Sebastian.

The guys looked confused, and Daisy grinned. "Just know if you meet someone in the state of Colorado, they are probably related to one of the two families in this room."

"You're not helping the situation," Noah said. "We're trying not to sound like we're a cult."

"But we are. But in a good sense." Daisy winked. "I need to head back to work, and I am so sorry I'm going to miss all of this, but have fun. It's good to meet you, Cassidy brothers. However, if you hurt my new best friend over here, I will have to hurt you. I'm trained." She winked as she said it, before she danced out, pulling Raven with her.

"Goodbye boys. I have to get back to work, too. Greer, keep me updated." They left quickly. I just shook my head, wondering how Daisy could do that. She looked so sweet and innocent, and she could take down a grown man twice her size without even breaking a sweat.

"We stopped by your shop, and they said that you were here," Heath said after a moment. "We heard a couple of interesting things from a friend of ours, thought we'd come and visit."

Greer looked at her brothers and frowned. "You could have called. It's this lovely century where we have cell phones that connect directly to each other. And we don't have data limits with our plans. I know I'm not on a family plan with you, but you still could have called."

There was something in her tone about that latter fact, and the brothers gave each other looks before they shook it off. I was missing something big here.

"Sorry, we just needed to get out of Portland," Luca said after a moment, but there was something in his voice, something that didn't have anything to do with Greer. Greer seemed to understand that, and she moved forward to hug her little brother, holding him tight.

"I'm sorry."

He kissed the top of her head, then looked at us. "Family drama, and well, life. Don't worry about us. I promise we aren't crazy. Well, not any crazier than you guys seem to be."

"I don't think that's saying much," Noah said, surprising a laugh out of me.

"Anyway," August began. "It seems that we are

making a mess of things. We just wanted to see you." He paused. "Mom and Dad came to visit, and we honestly didn't feel like staying. And then someone mentioned that you were dating these two, and well, here we are."

Greer froze, and while Noah didn't move his arm from her waist, I reached out and brushed my fingers along her arm. The brothers noticed the action, but they didn't seem to be judging anymore. Instead they appeared curious, maybe a bit protective.

"You should have called."

"We could have, but it is fun to annoy you," Heath said, his voice deadpan.

"I love you guys, but you seriously tend to overreact."

"Why don't you come over for dinner?" I blurted, and everyone looked at me, Greer's eyes wide.

"We don't want to intrude—" August began, and Greer burst out laughing.

"You just threw yourself into this situation without even calling. I know you guys have been messaging me daily to make sure I'm okay after the fire, and I will always love you for that, but you didn't need to come out."

"Our little sister almost died in a fire. Of course, we're going to come out as quickly as we could. I'm just sorry it took this long." August looked between us. "And, well, there seems to be other circumstances where we get to be the overprotective big brothers."

"Luca isn't even my big brother."

The youngest Cassidy narrowed his gaze. "I'm taller than you and have more muscle. That counts."

Greer rolled her eyes, and I cleared my throat again. "Seriously. Come over for dinner. And we'll actually have introductions that aren't posturing in the middle of Sebastian's shop."

"Yes, let's stop doing that," Sebastian said. "And as someone who has had family issues in the past, good luck," he said with a laugh as he moved away, leaving the three of us standing in front of the three Cassidy brothers.

"So, ink?" Luca asked, and Greer blushed.

"Yes. I thought it was time."

My phone buzzed, and I looked down. "I have to take this. I'm sorry."

"No problem. I know it's the middle of a workday."

"I work for Montgomery Security, the office next door. I'll be right back."

"We'll figure out dinner," Noah said with a shake of his head. "Because you know that we totally have groceries at the house."

Greer laughed, shaking her head. "I bought some this morning before I came in. Don't worry, I can cook something up."

"*We* can," I said, my phone buzzing again.

The three brothers began talking over each other, clearly curious, and I left them to it.

"Hello, Mrs. Price," I said as I answered.

"What took you so long?" Jocelyn Price asked, her voice breathy.

"I'm sorry, I was on another call," I lied. We had dropped Jocelyn Price the day before, Daisy having handled the communication. I wanted to deal with it myself, after all it had been my problem, but Daisy took it. She was just as tired of the situation as I was.

"I need you to come and work with me again. Please. I need your help."

The last time I went over there, she had been scantily dressed, pressing herself against me, all the while berating me for things I hadn't done.

This wasn't part of the job description, and I shouldn't have answered the call at all. But since I hadn't ended the contract myself, something had persuaded me to answer. I already regretted it.

"I'm sorry, Mrs. Price. But our contract has been terminated. We gave you a list of people you can work with."

"If you send Daisy over again, or if you don't come, I'll hurt myself. I promise I will."

I stiffened, on alert.

"Mrs. Price, please don't threaten to do something like that."

"I need you to help save me. Please. You don't know what I'll do."

She began to cry. I was walking into the office and put my phone on speaker and Jennifer looked up from her desk, eyes wide. She immediately pulled out her phone and I knew she was calling the authorities, as well as texting the group chat so everyone knew what was going on. We took these threats seriously, but fuck, I didn't know what I was supposed to do.

"Mrs. Price. Just sit down and breathe. You're going to be okay."

"I need you to come here."

"Someone will be there soon."

"Not someone, I need you."

Jennifer came to my side, recording the conversation. I wasn't sure what else we were supposed to do. We had been through something like this before, but nothing this serious. When I heard the sirens on the other end of the line, I wanted to feel relieved, instead my stomach churned.

It took over two hours for everything to get settled, during which most of the crew had come into the office to help. I had to speak with the authorities so they knew what was going on, and it appeared that Jocelyn Price was just fine. She had been ranting and drunk but hadn't had a weapon on her. But now everything was on file, and hopefully this would be the end of it. I wasn't sure what I was supposed to say, what else I was supposed to do. The authorities said I had done the right thing, staying on the line so she wouldn't hurt herself and calling for help. I didn't know if it was going to be enough, but I did know that there would be a restraining order in place soon. To protect her, and to protect me. To protect my team and family.

Daisy glared at the paperwork in front of her. "I can't believe she did this. There are people out there hurting, needing help, and she used that as a threat. I don't know what to say about that. It makes me sick."

I reached out and hugged her, forcing her to relax just a bit. "Everything will be okay."

"Are you lying to yourself or just me?"

"I'm not quite sure. But fuck, I think I'm late for dinner."

"Noah's with Greer and the brothers now, he hadn't wanted to leave her alone."

"I guess I have to go have dinner with the family."

"Well, you guys are together, living together, and raising a cat together. It's about time. She knows most of the Montgomerys and we know the Cages. It's time for you to know the Cassidys."

"I just don't want to analyze everything tonight."

"Then don't. Go over it later. But talk it over soon. Okay?"

"I guess. Fuck."

We went over a few more things, and then I headed back to the house, wondering what exactly I was going to walk into. I had kept Noah up to date in our texts, but I knew it wasn't enough. We were all going to have to sit down and go over a plan to make sure this never happened again.

That didn't make what was going to happen tonight any easier.

I walked inside the house after passing an unfamiliar rental SUV. It seemed the guys had flown into DIA, rented a car, and tried to find their sister. It was weird that they hadn't called, but then again, if my brothers were now living with two people that I didn't know, after nearly dying in a fire, I would've been out to wherever they were as soon as possible. And I knew the only reason they hadn't been out here as soon as the fire had happened was that Greer had yelled at them and said that she didn't want them there because she needed time to process.

I guess that time was up.

I walked inside to the scents of Italian food and garlic bread, and the sound of people laughing.

Immediately the tension in my shoulders eased slightly, and I found the five of them laughing and talking in the living room.

"You're here," Greer said as she walked towards me

and wrapped her arms around my waist. I relaxed and kissed the top of her head. "Hey. I'm here."

Horatio wrapped his little body around my legs and I bent down, my hand still in Greer's, to give love to the cat. "Hello boy."

"Everything okay?" Noah asked.

"Yeah." I looked towards Greer's brothers. "Sorry. Tough day at work."

"Noah mentioned some of it," Heath said, and I turned to Noah who shrugged.

"At least the stuff we could talk about. I'm sorry I wasn't there."

"The rest were, and I'm glad you were here. And I'm really glad that whoever cooked made what I think is garlic bread, because I'm starving."

Greer beamed. "It should be ready soon. Take a seat, and I'll get you some wine. Or do you want a beer?"

There was wine and beer on the table in front of everybody, and I sighed, rubbing my temples. "Maybe a beer, but I'll go get it. I could use some water too."

"I got it," Greer said, as she practically danced off, nervous tension riding her.

I looked at the brothers, not sure what I was supposed to do.

But it was August who broke the tension. "We're here to check on our little sister, she knows that, we know that, but not because of your relationship." I blinked as Noah stiffened on the couch.

August continued. "We're from Portland, we're good with poly relationships. And it's a new century, we're not here to judge. We are going to be the growly brothers who want what's best for our sister. But I don't know what Greer's told you about our family and how we were raised."

"I haven't," Greer said as she walked back into the living room, handing over a beer and a glass of water. I smiled, nodding in thanks, and she sat between Noah and me, clearly claiming her territory. When Horatio jumped on Noah's lap, I held back a laugh since the cat seemed to be doing the same.

"Our parents suck," Luca said with a shrug.

"Well, that's one way to put it," Greer said with a laugh

"Seriously, our parents were just on a sabbatical from their jobs because they wanted a honeymoon for their third marriage."

I frowned.

"Third marriage to each other," August clarified, and I just sat there, still confused.

"Our parents have been married three times, and divorced twice," Greer explained. "They really like the drama. They're back together again, and apparently just finished their honeymoon."

"The problem is, our parents like to play games," Heath added. "So, with each subsequent marriage and divorce, Dad got us because he wanted boys, and Mom got Greer."

I froze and looked between them. "They split you up?"

"In the worst version of the parent trap."

"And our parents did their best to make sure that we didn't get to see each other. Or get to know each other," Luca added, his voice soft.

"Jesus Christ," Noah whispered, and I agreed. I loved my family, I knew my brothers inside and out. They were everything. Yeah, we fought, we didn't get along all the time, but they were my brothers. And Greer had no one. Her brothers had each other, but she hadn't had anyone. No wonder she clung to her friends, and yet always seemed to be ready to walk out from our relationship because she didn't trust in it.

And right then I knew it was going to be harder than I thought to keep Greer. I already knew it was going to be hard to keep Noah, but hell, this was even harder now.

"Anyway, the parents are going on a year-long cruise," August said, with a wry eyeroll.

Greer stiffened, one hand on my knee, the other gripping Noah's. "Are you serious? What about the house? What about their jobs?"

"They got a settlement from Dad's job, and they can work remotely. They're selling the house. They're cutting all ties from Portland, according to Mom."

"But you guys live there. I thought with them being together again, Mom would want to be near you."

Heath laughed, but there was no humor in it. "Not so much. I think now that we are grown and out of their hair, they want to see how marriage and their drama can be without having to shuffle kids around. We wanted to see you though, because well, I'm really tired of our parents dictating our lives. Don't you think?"

Greer stood up and threw herself at her two closest brothers. They caught her quickly, and they all moved so they could hold her as she cried. I felt like a heel, because there was nothing I could do to make this better.

Her parents had truly fucked things up, and it seemed like all four of them needed each other, or at least a way to make this easier.

"Sorry for intruding on your life," August said gently. "We just wanted to see our sister. And we would've been out here sooner, but we had a few things to take care of."

Greer pulled back before sitting between us again, and Noah wrapped his arm around her shoulders as she wiped her tears away. "What did you need to take care of?"

The three brothers looked at each other, and then shrugged as one. A unit.

I didn't think Greer had even noticed at first, but she shrunk back at that. Because they had childhood memories and stories and inside jokes that she wouldn't. And her parents had done that to her.

I didn't know if I would ever meet them, but damn it, I wanted them to answer for it.

I met Heath's gaze, and the other man seemed to know exactly what I was thinking.

Well then.

"Well, there's really nothing holding us back now," Heath began.

Luca cleared his throat, a note of emotion in his voice as he spoke. "I don't think I want to go back. And since you're here, and our jobs mean that we can move anywhere, what do you say to your big brothers staying for a while? At least while we're able to set up shop."

"I have a few classes to take to make sure I can do that," August added.

Heath cleared his throat. "And there's an opportunity coming up for me. Seems like fate. Would you mind your brothers living near you? It's been a while since that happened," he added under his breath.

"And you're really okay with me living with Noah and Ford? And, well, *being* with them?" she asked. Noah let out a groan as I held back a laugh. That probably wasn't the best way to put that, and from the way the three brothers narrowed their gazes, I had a feeling that we were all on the same page.

"As long as they treat you right, we're not going to interfere," Luca said.

"And I don't think it's our right, yet," Heath added.

That wasn't how I thought tonight was going to go. But it had already been a damn long day.

"Well, I guess that means one more family to meddle?" Noah said.

"And our families haven't even really started yet," I added with a laugh, and then I let my worries slink out for the night.

There would be more to come, more stress, but we would deal with it.

And maybe, just maybe, with her brothers here, Greer would finally find a foundation to breathe again.

And trust.

I had a feeling it was going to be a lot harder than I had thought previously. But both Green and Noah were worth it.

Chapter 13
NOAH

"It's about time we did this," Ford said from my side, as we pulled our backpacks out of the back of the SUV.

I raised a brow at him as Greer sighed from beside us.

"Are you sure this is something you want to do?" I asked, and Greer winced.

"It's fine. I totally know what I'm doing. I'm even wearing the boots we broke in."

Ford and I glanced at each other, then down at Greer's new hiking boots. Her previous ones had been lost in the fire. She was slowly getting a new wardrobe, and new items to add to whatever had been in storage, but I knew times like this reminded her that she had lost some of herself. It hurt to think about, especially because we still didn't know what happened. The results of the investigation had been inconclusive.

They didn't know who started the fire, or if anyone had at all. And because it was inconclusive, the renter's insurance wasn't paying out, and her former landlords weren't letting her out of the lease. It was going to be a long haul to get through this, to fix it. And I knew she could do it on her own, but we were going to help. Even if she didn't want to let us.

Today, however, wasn't about that. It wasn't about anything except being us.

We had been seeing each other and sleeping together for nearly two months now. Living together, working near one another, and trying to figure out what the fuck we were doing.

Because of lack of time, we rarely went out on dates with just two people. It usually ended up being the three of us, like it was today.

I wasn't sure how to find the best way of being in a poly relationship. I didn't even think there was one. But I was going to figure it out, along with the two people at my side.

"Are you sure they're broken in enough?" Ford asked, a frown on his face.

"I wore them to work all this week. And I've been walking around with them, so the blister that I got the first day is now gone. It's fine. I promise. I even wore the good socks."

"I just don't want you to get hurt."

Greer smiled softly, then went on her tiptoes to give Ford a quick peck on the lips. "I'm fine. I promise. Now, I really hope your version of hiking is my version of hiking. I should have asked before, but I've been a little worried, so I have been living in a state of denial. It's been quite nice. You should visit."

I gave Ford a look, and the other man sighed. "Okay, it seems that your version of hiking might be Noah's version of hiking."

I closed the back of the SUV as we made our way towards the beginning of the trail. "My version of hiking includes going on a prescribed trail, bringing water and snacks, making it maybe a mile in, sitting and enjoying whatever view there is, and then making it back."

Greer burst out laughing, while Ford just sighed, shaking his head.

"What? I work out. I'm in shape. I'm good at what I do. But nature and I don't always get along. Do you see that, there's already a spider crawling on my foot." I gently kicked it off and held back a shudder.

It wasn't that I was afraid of spiders. But one had crawled on my face when I was a kid, and my brother hadn't said anything until I was talking to a girl that I liked, and it was a whole traumatic experience.

Of course, Ford had heard the story, and relayed it to Greer.

She reached out and gripped my hand, shaking her head. "I'm so sorry. Well, we could have done something different. Walk around the city."

"We do that every time I visit my mom. We're fine. Let's just enjoy this nature crap. And not get eaten by a bear."

"This is a whole new side of you. I didn't realize you didn't like hiking or the outdoors."

"I don't mind it. I enjoy the fresh air, and the views don't even feel real. Hell, every time we drive on I-25 and I look west, it looks like the mountains were fucking painted. It literally doesn't look real. I love it. However, every time I'm in it, something tries to kill me."

"That was one time," Ford said as he helped Greer over a fallen log.

"Which time? The time we went camping and I nearly fell off a cliff? Or the time that we went hiking and a deer nearly ran into me." I turned to Greer, she was holding back laughter. "Literally, the deer was running, and nearly ran into me. Could have killed me. But sure, nature's great."

"It's not that bad."

"Then there was another time that we were fucking around on the path behind my parents' house, and as I ducked Ford's fist, I fell right into an ant pile. And there

were a lot of ants. And as I brushed off the ants, screaming, a mosquito got my face. I don't even know how that
happened. But there we are. Nature hates me."

Greer stopped moving, bent over as she laughed, as
Ford joined her.

I shook my head at the two of them. "I work outside
all the time. I'm fine. I enjoy camping. I like going to
lakes and kayaking. When we went to Florida, and I
swam and I didn't see a shark, I figured nature was
great."

"And then he got stung by a jellyfish," Ford mock
whispered, and Greer had to wipe away tears.

"Oh my poor baby. I'm sorry." She reached forward
and cupped my cheek.

I swallowed hard, trying not to lean into the touch.
This was just temporary. I knew it. I wasn't going to keep
her, like I had said in bed that first time. Ford might, and
they'd be good together. But this was just a moment.
And I wasn't going to let myself feel more than was
necessary.

Even though that was a damn lie.

"We can go home if you want."

"I hear that challenge in your tone."

"Perhaps. Did I ever tell you about the time that I
went to the dunes with my brothers?" she asked as we
continued down the trail. I kept an eye out for any
animals or bugs that might want to murder me. Greer

and Ford would be safe. It didn't matter if a bear came at all three of us, it would come after me. I knew my lot in life.

"Which dunes?" Ford asked. He bumped into my shoulder, and I smiled at him. It was a good day, I liked being near them.

"It's off the Oregon coast, there are many dunes everywhere, I've even been to some really nice ones in Idaho."

"There's something in Idaho to see?" Ford asked. "I thought that was just potatoes."

"See, you live in this beautiful area, with nature and city life and everything you could possibly want, and you look down on the other states. I see you," Greer said with a laugh. "But the dunes that I'm talking about are on the Oregon coast. They're gorgeous, and you have to get down them to go to the beach. And depending on the time of the year, the beach is completely empty, glassy, and gorgeous."

"And like five degrees."

"There is that. But one time we went, it was a mile down the dunes, and you go through this little forested area as well, and we saw a few snakes."

I shuddered. "Really? See, nature's trying to kill you too."

"And they didn't even bother us. It was the second time I think that my parents were married, and things were going well. They went to a dinner of some sort, and my brothers and I decided to drive up the coast. We had a little bit of money, stayed at a really crappy hotel, but I felt so safe. We went to see the sea lion caves, and the noise and the smell was ridiculous, but it was so amazing. And we actually saw orcas try to eat seals. I'm pretty sure they got a couple, but we didn't know for sure, because they drag the seal or sea lion all the way down into the ocean to drown it. You don't see blood or anything."

Ford and I stopped and stared at her. "Are you serious right now?"

"It's the circle of life. I might have cried. But I'm trying not to think about that."

"And you saw these from the dunes?" I asked.

"No no. This was at the actual dune park, the same day, but two different areas of the coast. But anyway, you get all the way through there, and we saw a sea lion bob up into the waves, which was ridiculous because my youngest brother missed it. He was looking the other way when it happened and would never have believed us if we hadn't had video. But on the way back that was the issue."

"What do you mean?" Ford asked.

"You see, going down the dunes is ridiculous. It's hard, the sand's a little hot or cold depending on the weather, and it's a lot of work. Going up the dunes at nearly a seven-degree incline where the sand is constantly shifting underneath your feet? Impossible."

I pictured the sand dunes from the movies that I had seen and shook my head. "How the hell did you get up?"

"I cried and I cursed. I was a teenager, and I'm not the tallest person. My brothers have legs for days, and powered through by going up the dune. I however, didn't make it."

"Were you okay?" Ford asked.

"Eventually. But I was sweaty and the sand stuck to me. Every time I moved, I had to go on my hands and knees, so sand would go down my shirt. And then, my eldest brother did the worst thing possible."

"Did he push you down the dune?" I asked.

"No, though that probably would've been easier in the end. No, he came halfway down to stand by me and give me encouragement, and even offered to carry me back up."

I winced, knowing that would've stung. "And did you push him down?"

"If I could have without falling myself, I would have. It was embarrassing, and I made it back up eventually. But I was out of breath, and so thirsty I could barely breathe."

"How the hell do people get up those?"

"Well, usually people use the two-mile track to go up the back way; it's a nice flat and paved area. Not that I had seen that. And even if I had I wouldn't have done it."

I nodded, understanding. "Because then your brothers would've had to wait for you."

"Or they all would've gone with me, and I would've felt like a dork for not letting them go up on their own. Either way, that's my version of nature that tried to kill me. Oh, and I got bit by whatever bug lives in that sand. Little red marks all down my neck." She shuddered, and I reached out and gripped her hand.

"Let's not talk about bugs. I know they're coming for me."

"It's okay you two, I'll protect you."

Ford leaped over another log and helped Greer across.

"You slid down the embankment when we were visiting your brother's house that one day."

Greer looked between us, frowning. "What do you mean?"

"It was muddy, he had a cabin, and I decided to try to run up the hill. I fell. Hard. And slid all the way down the muddy embankment." Ford shook his head. "I also happened to fall down the snow path when we were sledding, using my face as a sled."

We continued to share horror stories of our deals with nature, the irony of us on a date in nature not escaping any of us.

We made it up the mile and a half trail, nodding at the other single hiker that had passed us. But other than that, there wasn't anyone else.

This was nice, different. And just for us.

I met Ford's gaze over Greer's head as we looked out at the scenery and I tried to breathe. No this wasn't a place to have any more fun than we already were. I could hear another group of hikers coming towards us. It was a little too busy for any fun in the trees.

"I can feel you guys looking over my head. What's going on?"

"Well, I was thinking about where to make out, but then I heard that other group coming," I answered.

Greer laughed. "We just finished discussing all of the horror stories of us in nature and you want to get partially naked? Yes, because some animal biting my ass when it's up in the air sounds amazing."

Ford held back his laughter as another set of hikers walked past, but I didn't, I threw my head back, letting the laugh hit me hard.

"The only thing biting your ass is going to be one of us," I whispered, my lips right at her ear. "I promise."

"Damn straight. But, this is beautiful. And I'm glad we're doing it."

"Yeah? Me too."

"So, did you guys always know you were going into

business together?" she asked as we sat and snacked on trail mix.

My feet dangled off the side of a rock, but we weren't anywhere close to a cliff. Frankly I didn't trust us.

Ford was the one who answered. "I always knew that I wanted to go into something like it. I watched Noah's dad kick ass at it, and I don't know, it just seemed right. We went to college to make sure that we knew how to run a business, to see if there was anything else we wanted to do, but this just made sense."

"Plus, I like owning the business. It was just our luck that three of my family members wanted to join in, so the initial costs weren't too bad for each of us."

"It's nice that you all work together, that you have this family business." She paused. "Although, I guess you're not a Montgomery," she said slyly to Ford.

"No, though we work with my family too. So I didn't completely forsake them for the enemy."

"Do they see it like that?" Greer asked, and we both shook our heads.

"There's not a Cage and Montgomery rivalry. I promise," I answered.

"No not even a little. Though I am surprised that none of my brothers have dated your sisters or cousins yet."

"Well, we don't know everything. But let's not put that out into the universe," I answered.

"Why wouldn't you?"

"Because things get complicated." I looked at Ford as I said it, but thankfully he changed the subject so we didn't have to go down that road.

"Anyway, I like being able to work with my friends. I like what we do."

"It's the same with me. I love that Raven and I had this idea and we actually made it work. I know moving out to Colorado to do it seems extreme, but this was her home, and I needed a change."

I trailed my thumb along her knuckles and thought for a moment. "This is your home now. Are you okay with your brothers making it theirs?"

"I think so. I love them, I just don't know them as well as I want to."

"This would give you the opportunity. And, I don't know, maybe they need it too."

"Maybe. They've been through a lot. Different than me, but a lot. Although this does mean I'll have three growly brothers constantly trying to watch out for me." She met both of our gazes, and I laughed.

"Well, they can just add to the queue. It's a little ridiculous at this point."

We sat there for a bit longer, watching birds and other animals go past us.

This was nice, it felt good.

It felt real.

But as Greer leaned her head on Ford's shoulder, the two of them talking about an upcoming movie, I just sat back. The two of them would work well together. Yes, we were making it work for now, but I knew one day they might not want this anymore, so I would have to be the one to walk away. It would keep things simpler. And we could still remain friends.

If I kept lying to myself, it would make sense.

I wouldn't break.

Chapter 14
GREER

A HAND SLIPPED OVER MY HIP, AND I SMILED OVER MY shoulder at a very familiar man. Ford lay there, his hair a mess, his eyes squinting since he didn't have his contacts in.

"Good morning," I whispered.

"Good morning. Did Noah wake you when he left to head to the project house?" he asked, his voice a low rumble.

I shook my head and pressed back into him. His very hard erection nudged at my backside, and I wiggled my hips to press against him more.

He groaned. "Naughty."

"You're the one with the steel pipe pressed against my ass."

"Well, I can't help it, you're naked and sliding against me. But I guess this is what happens when we all fall asleep in a pile together."

The night before I had been working on paperwork, going through a thousand things that were required when you were a business owner. Ford had worked late, dealing with another project, while Noah had been working on paperwork to help out one of his siblings. When Ford finally made it home, we all kept working on our own individual things, before we eventually put on a movie and ended up tangled together on the couch. Then we'd moved to the bedroom. And while I was slightly sore from the night before, I was always ready for him.

I had been with Noah and Ford separately, and together. We had been together in every way possible, in pairs and all together. This felt right, as if we were making sense of it all, and falling into a routine that worked.

But I didn't want to think too positively about it, or too hard. Because I was afraid of what would happen when it ended.

So I didn't think.

Instead, I tilted my chin so I could capture his lips.

He groaned and smiled against my lips. "Well, that's one way to wake up."

"I know of another." Pushing all worries out of my mind, I slid my hand between us and squeezed the base of his shaft. He rocked his hips as he slid his dick against the crease of my ass.

"Damn it."

"Ford, I need you."

"You've got me."

There was something about the way he said that, something I wanted to know more about, but I just let him kiss me as he slid his hand between my legs, pleasuring me with just a bare touch. His other hand was wrapped around me, lazily playing with my nipple, cupping my breast. I still had my hand on his crotch, and we rocked against each other until he pulled away and grabbed a condom from the bedside table. Wrappers littered the floor from the night before, and we were going to have a long morning cleaning up. But those thoughts didn't linger.

He wrapped the condom around his dick and I lifted my leg, keeping my back to him. Even at this angle, I could meet his gaze, and he parted his lips, slowly sliding deep inside me. When he was balls deep, filling me to every inch of pleasure, I shivered. I rocked back, and he groaned, before he moved.

It was a lazy love making, and it was everything that I could ever want.

"Yes. Yes," I whispered.

"Come for me. Come for me, Greer. Squeeze my dick, show me how much you want me."

"I'll always want you." I hadn't meant to say that, but he smiled against me, nibbling at my shoulder before he captured my lips again.

I came then, but he didn't. He pulled out of me, and I felt the loss, before he had me on my back and was sliding deep inside me again. I wrapped my arms around him, one leg around his waist. Then he moved me again, pressing my knee to my shoulder, and I was grateful for my yoga classes. He grinned as he pounded into me, and I moaned for him, needing more.

I could easily spend every morning for the rest of my life like this. With Ford, with Noah. With both.

I knew that it was a dream, that wouldn't happen, but I didn't care right then. I just needed him.

And when Ford rocked his hips in just the perfect way, sending me over the edge again, I pushed out all thoughts of what was wrong, what couldn't be, and just thought of him—and the man I knew we both loved.

Later, after we showered, we were laughing around the kitchen as I made a quick espresso for both of us to take to work.

"Did you want me to drive us in?"

We had taken to carpooling as much as possible. All of our friends and most of my regulars knew that I was seeing both of them. They also knew that I was living with them, and working in the same damn building. It would've felt like too much, except that during the day we rarely saw each other. I knew the guys didn't even work side by side most days. We all had things to do, and focused on what we needed to. We were business owners, we needed to put business first. Though while our nights didn't always end at the same time, we ended up tangled together more often than not.

Three nights ago in fact, knowing that the guys had a hard day and I had an early morning, the guys had slept together, and I listened to them from my room. I had smiled, using my hand to send myself over. I knew they hadn't been loud on purpose, that was just them. And I liked that they had time to themselves. Just like I had this morning alone with Ford. And earlier in the week I'd had time with Noah.

We weren't just a unit, we were parts of units all blended and tangled together. It was a perfect knot, one I was truly afraid would come unraveled if I thought too hard. So I wouldn't let myself.

I grinned and grabbed my bag. "Yes, carpooling would be good. The employee parking lot in the back is getting a bit crowded."

Ford winced. "Yes, and it's only going to be worse when we open up the other two units."

"When is that going to be complete?"

"There was a setback with one of the permits—we're in the middle of an election season, so things slid through the cracks on their end. But you know the Montgomerys will fix it."

"And if they don't, the Cages will swoop in," I teased.

"Don't even joke. You know my brothers would buy this business. They're real estate developers after all. Well, at least some of them. Some of them do other things."

"So I hear. Though I have a feeling they've been very careful about not coming into my café," I said as we got into the SUV.

Ford blushed. "Well, yes. I sort of warned them away."

I frowned, wondering why a little sense of unease slid over me. Ford pulled out of the driveway before he looked over at me and shook his head. "Not that. I'm not ashamed or anything. I swear. They all know what's going on. Well, at least as much as I want them to know," he said with a wink. "It's more about, with some of Noah's family and your friends working all in the same building, it can be a lot. And my brothers are a lot." There was more happening beneath the surface than I could process right then. I figured I would find out more soon.

"So you're not ashamed of me," I said, only partially teasing.

We were at a stoplight, so Ford gripped my hand and forced me to look at him.

"Not at all. I'm not ashamed of you, or what we have together and with Noah. I swear. It's more that I want you to myself as much as possible. Well, to ourselves," he corrected with a smile.

I wasn't sure what I was supposed to say, but fortunately the light turned green and he squeezed my hand again before he looked back to the road. "Either way, I don't think I'm able to hold them off for much longer. We may have to do dinner or something."

I gulped. "Oh?"

So far I had managed not to do dinners with either of the big families. The fact that we'd had dinner with my family had been an accident. Mostly because my brothers had ambushed us. And when and if they moved here, it would be more often. But for now, the big family dinners had been avoided, and I was grateful for that. I needed time to figure out what was going on, even though I hadn't actually figured that out.

We had done group events, where we hung out at a bar or a Rockies game together, and it had felt normal. Mostly because we all practically worked together.

But dinner? That felt serious.

"You don't have to if you don't want to," Ford said, a casualness in his tone that implied the opposite.

"Of course, I want to. I'm just trying to think of what to wear. What I'm supposed to say. I've never actually had dinner with the family before. Which sounds weird now that I've said that aloud."

"The only family dinners I've ever had beside my own were with Noah's. And we were just friends then. So don't worry, we'll all feel under the microscope. It's going to be fun."

He pulled into the employee parking lot and winked at me. "We'll figure it out."

I nodded. "Yes. We will."

I just had to hope I would figure out what I was doing before then.

WORK WAS HECTIC, and had a few blowups that made me feel like I was losing my mind.

"What do you mean you don't have it?" I asked my supplier.

"I don't have it because you canceled the order. I have the form right here."

I stared at the form he was showing me and shook my head. "No. I would never have signed that. We need the supplies."

"And you have what you ordered."

I stared at the signature again. "That's not my signature. Who signed?"

The guy looked down at the form and shrugged. "I don't know. It wasn't me who got it. It was my team. And your team signed for this order. The rest was canceled. I thought it was odd, but when you didn't call to change, I assumed that was right. Not quite sure what I can do for you right now."

"Are you serious right now, Robert?" I asked as I ran my hands over my face.

"I don't know what to tell you. You need to talk to your staff members, because I have the page right here. But, this is your signature, so either they're falsifying documents for you, or you had too much caffeine and you don't remember."

He laughed as he said it, that annoying lecherous laugh that I tried to ignore. We had three different suppliers that we had contracted with, and I liked Robert the least. But damn it, we really needed him.

"Okay, give me what you have."

"You're looking at it," he said to the six boxes at my feet.

I wanted to scream, but that wouldn't accomplish anything. He already thought I was a hysterical woman, so I was just going to have to deal with it.

He left without another word, and I looked over at Raven, who scowled.

"What the hell?"

"I don't know, but something's going on and we'll figure it out. We just don't have time right now. Fuck, this is going to screw up inventory, and our next big catering order."

"We'll have to make do, or find another supplier. But that's not my signature." I pointed to the sheet, and she nodded. "It's not. But somebody thought it was. Someone's playing games and I don't like it."

One of our team members called from the front counter, and Raven sighed before she went back to work, squeezing my hand.

I just stood there wondering how the hell this had all blown up.

It had been a long morning already, and I just wanted to go home. But of course, I couldn't. No, I had to be a boss and actually run the business I owned because I thought it was a good idea.

I kept going, working order after order, trying to take notes of what inventory we were missing, all while wondering what could have possibly happened with the order.

But when I heard the sound of metal hitting metal, my head shot up.

"What are you doing?" I asked.

Jeff winced. "I don't know. It's just making that clinking noise."

"Don't touch it," I said as quickly as possible, trying to sound calm as I practically ran towards my baby. My espresso maker.

I scowled at the top of it, the gleaming machine that I had taken months to pick out.

"Oh my God," I whispered.

"What is it?"

"There's a piece missing."

I looked around, dropped to the ground, and sighed when I saw the piece on the floor, before scowling up at Jeff.

"Did you drop this?"

"No, I promise. It might have been loose though. I don't know. I swear."

The man looked close to tears, and I shook my head, sighing.

"It was an accident." Though I wasn't quite sure about that. Not with how my day was going. "It should be easily fixed. Just give me a minute."

"I'm seriously sorry, Greer."

"It's fine. I promise." I did not know if I was lying, but I let it go and quickly fixed the machine. Everything looked to be in working order, but as soon as the shift was over, I would go over everything again.

What the hell was going on with this day? It was one thing after another.

"You have visitors," Raven said from the front of the store, and I smiled, making my way to the guys.

"Hey," I said, feeling flustered, sweaty, and a mess.

"What's wrong?" Ford asked, as Noah tilted his head, studying me.

"Nothing," I said, as I pushed my hair back from my face before going to wash my hands. "Just a long day. What can I get you?"

"I already took their order. You should go take a break."

I scowled at my best friend. "I don't need a break. I just need *something* to go right."

"Come on, tell us about your day," Noah said.

Ford grinned and picked up the cookie Raven handed him.

"Smells amazing."

He took a bite, swallowed, then his eyes widened.

Everything happened in slow motion. Ford dropped the cookie and coughed, rubbing his throat.

"Oh my God, what's going on?" Raven asked.

"Did that have cashews in it?"

Ford was highly allergic to cashews, so we never had them in the store. Not with any of our milks, flours, or nuts. We even sourced from a company that was allergy friendly, and understood how to keep materials separate.

"No, of course not. We don't have cashews here."

Ford reached in his pocket, his hands shaking.

I put my fingers between my lips and whistled.

"Somebody call an ambulance."

"Do you have your EpiPen?" Noah asked as Ford's face turned red, bright red splotches covering his arms and neck.

Fear pummeled me, but I ran towards him, forcing him to sit down.

"What can we do?" I asked Noah.

"I need a fucking EpiPen."

He pulled the pen out of Ford's pocket and looked at him.

"Are you ready?"

Ford's eyes widened, and I could hear Raven on the phone behind me, talking quickly to the 911 dispatcher.

I gripped Ford's hand, not knowing what I was supposed to do, feeling helpless.

Noah flicked the cap off and stabbed Ford's thigh. I didn't even know how to use an EpiPen, but that was something I was going to learn. Noah knew what he was doing, thank God, and when Ford was able to take a deeper breath, the EpiPen working quickly, I hoped it was enough.

"I'm okay," Ford rasped, before his eyes drooped and he slumped against me.

"What's going on?"

"He's breathing, but let's get him on the ground, just in case."

Raven and my team were handling the others, as I held Ford close, his eyes fluttering as he took raspy breaths.

I didn't know if the EpiPen was going to last long, or what else needed to happen, but Noah seemed to.

He was talking to someone on his phone quickly, then scowling down at the cookie.

Raven was crying, and I just looked at her, wondering what I was supposed to do.

Then the paramedics walked in, and Noah pulled me away, letting the EMTs work.

"Is he going to be okay?" I asked.

"He's going to be fine. Accidental contamination like this happens. That's why he carries the EpiPen."

"But we don't have cashews in this building. We always double check."

"Noah," Raven said from my side. "I don't know what happened, but I'm so sorry."

I held him close while reaching out to grip my best friend's hand.

"We should follow the ambulance. Okay?"

I nodded as I undid my apron and handed it to Raven.

"We'll handle it here. Just be with him."

I had no idea how cashews had even gotten near that cookie. But maybe something had happened with the supplier, or someone had brought in a cookie of their own, or someone had brought in nuts and bumped into Ford. I didn't know, but we would find out.

Ford had almost died. We had almost lost him.

We got into Noah's truck and I gripped his hand, trying to believe everything would be okay.

Even though I wasn't sure that was possible.

Chapter 15
FORD

I HAD NEVER RIDDEN IN THE BACK OF AN AMBULANCE before. Considering my job, and the fact that I had been shot at, that was quite surprising.

But in the hour since my throat closed up, where not even a whiff of oxygen could get through, I'd had time to think about what could have fucking happened.

It still shocked me, that sense of helplessness. I hadn't been able to get my own EpiPen. When I was younger I had thought it annoying that I always had to have it on me. My other friends who were allergic to things only needed Benadryl or a nose spray in order to be okay. Or they just broke out into hives and quickly showered. Me? Not so much. I had to use the EpiPen once when I was a kid, but we had been close to a hospital, and my dad had carried me the block to get there. Because every time you used an EpiPen, you needed to see a doctor. It was only a stopgap measure, one that sent chemicals straight through your body trying to counteract the allergens. And my body felt like I had been run over by a two-ton truck.

I still remember my dad holding me, the fear in his gaze. Mom had been running behind him, all six of my brothers trailing her. My dad was a large man, strong, and a little intimidating.

He had to be with so many boys. My mom was the same. They still were, although I didn't see them as much as I wanted to. Dad was constantly traveling for work, and Mom had a thousand other duties that had nothing to do with me.

We were adults now, living our own lives, but the family text chat had blown up once Noah took my phone and called my eldest brother.

Mom: *We're on our way.*

Flynn: *Damn straight.*

Dad: *Don't curse in the family group chat.*

Hudson: *How many of us do you want there? How many do they even let back in the room?*

Dorian: *Does it matter? We're going.*

James: *Fucking right.*

Theo: *No cursing.*

Mom: *I know you're mocking your father. Stop.*

Aston: *Everyone stop annoying Ford. I don't even know if he has his damn phone. Sorry for cursing. I'll organize everything.*

After that, the family group had gone quiet. Aston was dealing with everyone, and I didn't know how many Cages would show up.

Currently in my room though were the two people I wanted to see more than anything.

"Thanks for my phone," I rasped, gesturing with it towards Noah.

Noah sat by my side, a frown on his face. "You dropped it. You know, when you scared the shit out of me."

Greer stared at me, her teeth biting into her lower lip.

I wanted to say that was sexy, but she looked so damn scared.

So I reached out, and though I couldn't actually touch her, she seemed to understand what I wanted and slid her hand into mine.

"I'm fine. I'm going to go home soon."

"Is that what the doctor said? Because my shop almost killed you."

She wasn't crying, though I knew she had. Damn it, I never wanted to see her cry.

Noah wrapped his arm around her shoulder, bringing her close, and something inside me settled. They would be fine. No matter what, they would be fine.

"Your shop didn't almost kill me."

"Something got cross-contaminated, and you had an allergic reaction where you needed to use an EpiPen. That seems pretty close to death to me."

I met Noah's gaze, but he didn't back me up. I frowned before Noah seemed to get it.

"It wasn't your fault, though I would like to know how the cashews got there."

"I have no idea. I've been having problems with the supplier, so maybe something got mixed in? But I don't know."

"Kane is there helping Raven check everything out, and they're going to dump most of the stock."

Greer paled, but nodded. "Good. That's good."

"No it fucking isn't," I growled. "You don't have to do that."

"Yes I do. What if something else is in there? What if there's a cashew somewhere in the building, and you get sick again? We pride ourselves that we can have gluten-free products, and certain nut allergy safe items. Not everything, as it's impossible, but with at least what we are able to. So yes, we're going to dump what we have, but oddly enough, we didn't have much because there was an issue with the paperwork."

She explained it to me and I frowned, looking at Noah who just shook his head tightly. Oh we would talk about that later of course. Because something wasn't adding up here.

Between that issue, the random broken pieces of equipment, and now this?

Something was going on, and I didn't know what.

We'd figure it out, and though I had gotten hurt this time, Greer was dealing with the consequences. And damn it, she had gone through enough. She didn't need to deal with this too.

Something prickled in the back of my memory, trying to remember something else that could be connected, but before I could figure it out, the door opened and a familiar face stepped through.

Big brother Aston was as tall as me, not as wide, but just as strong. While I had a beard, he was clean-shaven for now, though sometimes he sported a beard. His hair was a little longer on the top, clean cut at the sides. He looked like a business mogul, which he was.

He had on dress pants and a button-up shirt, but no tie or suit jacket. Either he had taken it off on the way here, or this was his casual look for the day.

Flynn stood behind him, brow raised.

Flynn was the second eldest, though his twin, Hudson, always joked that Flynn seemed like the youngest.

Flynn was also dressed in a suit, including a tie and

jacket, and I had a feeling he had come straight from whatever board meeting with the site planners he was in.

They worked together and were a damn good team, but currently looked as if they wanted to tear someone's head off.

"Hey there," I said slowly, staring at my brothers. "How did you get back here? I thought we were only allowed to have two people in?" I asked.

"We have our ways. Although fending off the entire family was not easy. So be happy it's just the two of us, and not Mom and Dad and the rest of the crew. There would be wailing if there was."

My mom wasn't prone to hysterics, but if one of her baby cubs got hurt, she turned into a mama bear. And my mom, while sweet and amazing sometimes, was not always nice to those in her path when it came to her kids.

I cleared my throat when I noticed Greer stiffen in her chair. She was still wearing her work clothes, and her hair was piled on the top of her head, and she had been crying. I thought she was the most beautiful woman I'd ever seen in my life. But I knew she probably wasn't happy meeting my family like this.

I sat up as much as I could in my hospital bed. "Aston, Flynn, I know you guys already know Noah, but this is Greer."

Aston studied Greer for so long without saying

anything, I was about to slide right out of this bed and beat the shit out of my brother. From how Noah glared, he felt the same way.

But it was Flynn who moved forward.

"Hello there. We've heard so much about you, and our dearest brother's been hiding you. I guess it does take an act of God or an actual ambulance ride for us to be able to meet you."

He held out his hand as Greer stood up, her lips twitching. "If it helps, I haven't met all of the Montgomerys. I hear that's a little scary."

"I would say we're scarier, but it'd be kind of fun to see who wins." Flynn winked, flirting as usual. I scowled at my brother as he brought Greer's hand to his mouth and kissed her knuckles.

"So lovely to meet you."

Greer blinked at him, then looked over at me. "So I guess it's all of you then."

I burst out laughing, even though I was exhausted.

Aston sighed. "Sorry, when my baby brother is hurt, I turn into the asshole everyone thinks I am. Hello, it's nice to finally meet you. Even under these circumstances." He shook her hand, and then glared at me. "You seriously shouldn't have been hiding her."

"We're taking our time. You know there's been a lot going on."

Aston nodded. "Seems like. I really am sorry about

the fire. If there's anything you need from our side of the family, let us know," Aston began.

Greer blushed. "I was renting before, and well, don't worry about me. The guys have been taking care of me." She blushed, then put her hands over her face before letting out a small scream. "I'm usually better at people. I'm a freaking barista. It's what I do. Sorry."

This time Flynn joined my laughter. Noah just shook his head, a silent sentinel behind her.

"We can head out and go get something to eat if you guys want some time alone with your brother." Noah looked at me, and I smiled at him. Noah always knew what to say. And hell, he knew my family just as well as I did. We had been best friends for so long, we didn't have secrets.

"No, how about we just wait to see how long you're going to be in? And then we'll all go get some food together."

I nodded at Aston's recommendation. "That sounds like a plan to me."

"You will be resting though," Greer warned. "Don't think because you can laugh it off that means you can pretend that this didn't happen. I watched you almost suffocate, so you're going to have to lie there while we feed and pamper you. You didn't let me do anything on my own after the fire. So you're going to have to just sit back and let us take care of you."

"What she said. Though she said it much nicer than I would have," Noah added.

I looked at them and knew that, damn it, I loved them. Both of them. This was going to be so fucking complicated.

But from the way that my brothers looked between us, a small smile playing on Flynn's lips and a guarded expression on Aston's face that I couldn't read, I had a feeling there'd be no hiding my feelings for long.

And I wasn't sure if I wanted to hide them at all. Despite the consequences.

IT DIDN'T TAKE LONG for me to get discharged, for which I was grateful. My car was in the garage when we pulled in, as Kane had brought it home for me. I'd have to text him later to thank him, but I was exhausted.

They set me up on the couch, Greer ordering everybody about, and I smiled as my two big brothers moved around, doing exactly what she asked. Noah following her orders was a given—we would do anything for her—but the fact that Aston and Flynn were now eating out of her hand?

Oh yeah, I liked it.

Greer went about making dinner, deciding that she wanted to cook to busy herself, and Flynn went to help her, while Noah dealt with a call from work.

That left my eldest brother sitting in the chair next to me, giving me a look I couldn't quite read.

"What?" I asked, too tired to deal with whatever was going on.

"You guys seem happy."

I frowned, having not expected that.

"We are. I mean, we're getting there."

"I thought this was just fun. I thought that you were just going to see what would happen if you shared with your best friend."

I blushed, then looked over Aston's shoulder to make sure that Greer and the others couldn't hear.

"It was never like that. Greer's different."

"I can tell. I like the way the two of them balance each other out, and you. I'm not saying this is going to be easy, but I see Noah's parents. I know it can work. Noah's always been special. He's always been one of us."

"Don't let his family hear you say that," I whispered, rubbing a hand over my chest.

"Do they know you love them?"

I shook my head, grateful that Aston's voice was barely audible.

"They're going to figure it out soon. Are you going to be okay if it takes them longer to figure it out?"

"Why would you say that?" I asked, my throat tight again but it had nothing to do with allergies.

"Because love is complicated. It's supposed to be the

easiest thing you do, but that's bullshit and we all know it."

"Have you ever been in love?" I asked, surprising myself. I knew he had relationships before, you couldn't hit your mid-thirties and work with people as much as my brother did and not. But I wasn't sure.

Aston smiled. "Maybe. Maybe not. But this isn't about me."

"Evasive."

"Maybe. It doesn't matter though, because we are talking about you. Just be safe, okay? I like them. Both of them. I don't have answers for you. And I like knowing what will happen."

"And you can't always predict that. But I'll be okay. Once we get through this, and figuring out who we are together, it'll work."

I had such conviction in my voice because it had to work.

My brother nodded, studying my face. "Well then, I'm going to go see what your lovely woman is cooking for us, and make sure that Flynn isn't burning it."

I laughed, shaking my head as Noah walked into the living room.

"Everything okay?" I asked.

"Everything's fine, but the Montgomerys have heard that the Cages have met Greer, so now we are being summoned."

Aston smiled wide for the first time that afternoon, and my shoulders shook with laughter.

"What did you say?" Greer asked as she came out into the living room, a platter of appetizers in her hands, Flynn holding twice as much in his.

"We're going to a Montgomery dinner. Sorry, I can't hold them off any longer. They're worried about Ford of course, but they also want to see you." Noah leaned down and took the platter from Greer's hands before giving her a kiss on the cheek.

Greer rolled her eyes. "I suppose it's about time."

"Gird your loins, y'all," Flynn said as he set down the platter, and I laughed, wondering why this felt like family, why it felt right.

Hoping to hell this was only a beginning.

Chapter 16
NOAH

"WHY DID I LET MY FAMILY BULLY ME INTO THIS?" I asked as I turned down the street towards my parents' place. This wasn't the home we had grown up in. In fact, because part of my extended family built new homes and restored older homes, we moved—within the same school district—a few times growing up. Every time we expanded as a family, we increased in the size of the home. It had been needed, because my parents also needed two bedrooms, so they had space for each other and themselves. And my father, Jake, needed space for his art and workshop. At one point, my dad, Border, had actually worked from home as well, since it was easier raising four of us. Everybody had done their best to make sure that we never felt left out or alone. The fact that my mom could also make her own schedule had helped.

But now we were going to a place that I had never lived. My parents wanted to downgrade, because they hadn't needed the huge house after we started moving out, and though they joked about grandkids, my parents were never the kind to beg for them or annoy their kids about it.

So now only my youngest two siblings still lived with my parents, while both Skylar and I lived on our own.

And yet, it didn't matter, because this was home.

"Why are you nervous? I'm the one meeting your entire family all at once."

"It's just his parents and siblings. You're not meeting the aunts and uncles and cousins and grandparents," Ford said with a laugh. "That would get awkward."

I looked in the rearview mirror at Ford, who just winked at me, and shook my head.

Ford was still a little tired from the epinephrine, but that was fine. I wasn't going to let him work too hard or move around much. And neither was my family. He thought his brothers were bossy? He should have known better.

"And we're not allowed to bring anything? Are you sure? I hate showing up empty handed."

I reached out and gripped Greer's hand. "Mom said not to. And this way when we invite them over, and we say don't bring anything, they won't. We only bring things over if we want to make sure that we get to eat a certain item."

"So if I say I'm gluten-free, I make sure that I bring something I can eat."

"True, but we also try to make sure that we actually have something for people who are gluten-free." I paused. "You know, there are some members of the family who are dairy-free, allergic to cheese. Those people, well, they have to bring their own food."

I said it so seriously, that Greer just blinked at me while Ford burst out laughing.

"Oh, I've heard about your family and cheese. I thought it was just a joke."

"It is. But they really do like all kinds of cheeses. There will be at least one cheese plate at this dinner by the way. Even if it doesn't go with the rest of the meal, there will be cheese."

"Cheese goes with every meal. Maybe not an Irish cheddar with every meal, but we can always find something. I know you like cheese because you nibble off the same block I do."

Greer blushed. "I can't help it. I like cheese."

"You're going to fit right in with the Montgomerys," Ford said dryly as I pulled in front of the house.

I sat a moment, steeling myself, but then the door opened and my mom came out, waving.

"You know, I've seen your mom before, she's come into the shop. But I haven't met her since I moved in. Can I just say she's gorgeous?"

I laughed and nodded. "Go ahead and tell her that. She always likes to hear it."

"Also, I feel like I need to get more ink."

"Don't say that around them," I said before I opened my car door. "Because as it is, she's already going to bug you to make sure that she gets into the rotation."

Ford kept laughing as he got out of the car, opening up his arms to hug my mom tight. But Greer frowned at me.

"What do you mean?"

"Sebastian got to you first. Well, now my mom will want a turn. Her siblings all take turns between her and her brother, Austin. They own the original Montgomery Ink," I explained. "And with each generation comes a new responsibility," I said seriously, as she rolled her eyes and got out of the car.

I grinned and got out after her, locking the door behind me.

"Are you sure you're okay? We've got the armchair all ready for you, with a lap blanket."

Ford rolled his eyes. "Seriously? I'm fine. I could do a cartwheel."

"No you won't," both Greer and my mom said at the

same time. Then they looked at each other and burst out laughing.

I pinched the bridge of my nose, wondering if introducing my girlfriend to my mother was a good idea.

Girlfriend. Holy hell, had I just thought the phrase girlfriend? Maybe I had. I looked at Ford. That meant my best friend was now my boyfriend. Well hell. What was I supposed to do with that?

"Stop monopolizing the kids and come inside," my dad, Jake, said as he waved us in.

I could hear my siblings behind him, wanting to get out and meet Greer and Ford, as if they hadn't known Ford for years, and they had all met Greer at her shop.

But this was different, way different.

My mom had her arm around Greer's shoulder, her free hand holding Ford's, as she led them into the house, leaving me behind.

"Seriously? Not even a hello to your favorite son?"

"Not so favorite anymore," my brother Cooper called out.

I flipped him off, as my father, Border, shook his head. "Be nice. At least when you're on the front lawn. We don't want our neighbors to think we are insane."

"I think that ship sailed long ago," my little sister Naomi said.

Skylar moved forward, pushing my dads out of the way, everybody introducing themselves all at once, speaking over each other, laughing, and feeling as if they had been friends for eons.

I stood back, watching as everyone tucked Ford into the armchair, including a lap blanket. He let them, but sighed happily when my dad handed over a beer.

"Excuse me, should you be drinking?" Naomi asked, tapping her foot.

"Yes, I'm allowed to. Plus your dad gave it to me. It seems only right. I don't want to offend my boyfriend's dad."

Everybody froze for a minute, Ford's words on the same lines as my thoughts.

"It's about damn time," Jake muttered as Border laughed softly.

My mom and Skylar had pulled Greer around the house, giving her a tour. Cooper sidled over to me.

"So. Meeting the parents?"

I narrowed my gaze at my brother. "You're a menace."

"Not as much as you. Following in the family footsteps. I'm so proud." Cooper wiped a fake tear, and I pushed at his shoulder.

"Don't test me."

"Don't push your brother," my mom said from the hallway, even though her back was to me.

"Seriously, how does she see things like that?" I asked, but my father, Border, just grinned.

"That's your mom. She's damn good at that. Now, we have cheese in the fridge, and I didn't ask if Greer ate cheese."

"She does. Don't worry, I would've sent out the alarm if she was dairy-free."

"Hey, I married into this family, I know how scary it is." Border said with a laugh, as he and I walked to the kitchen to start pulling the food out.

"This is a lot of food," I said, then narrowed my gaze at him. "It is just us right? You didn't invite the rest of the family?"

"Don't worry. We're enough to scare anyone. But you know what? I like this look on you. The three of you."

"I didn't actually mean for this to happen."

"I think you and Ford have always been on this collision course." At my stunned gaze, he smiled and continued. "We've all seen it. We all let you be. We may pretend to meddle and to be in everyone's business, but we're not annoying about it."

I nodded. "You're right. You guys let us be, let us grow."

"We try our best," he said with a laugh, unwrapping the platter and setting it on the island. Cooper walked by and plucked a piece of cheese before we even finished.

I shook my head, wondering why I didn't visit more often. Yes I was here at least twice a month, but we needed to do it more. Or maybe I was just hiding. Not that I wanted to think too hard about that.

"I think Greer is what pushed you over the edge, at least from an outsider's perspective."

"I don't know. It all just happened. I'm really afraid that it's just going to stop happening without me consciously knowing."

My dad gripped my shoulder and squeezed. "I don't think that's going to be a problem. I think you guys just need to remember to communicate. You know, it's funny, your dad and I dated before we even met your mom."

I grinned, remembering the story. "Well, Ford and I never really dated. We've just been friends."

"I don't really want to hear the details of what the two of you were doing before the three of you became a three. But here's some unsolicited advice," he continued after I finished laughing. "Talk. Don't bottle it up. If you don't communicate what you're feeling, and what needs to happen, it's not going to happen. Communication is key when it comes to two people in a relationship, but add a third person? You're not just adding one more connection, you're adding countless others. It's the dynamics of how you work as a unit, how you work separately, and how you work as pairs within the three. It's complicated, it's not always easy, and you're going to fight. But making up is fun too." He winked as he said it, and I quickly pushed images out of my mind.

"Really?"

"Really." He gripped my shoulder again. "I want you to be happy. And from what I can tell, they make you happy. I know you're all going through a lot, and you're still at the beginning of the relationship, but think about what you want, and make sure you tell them. Don't hide from it because you're afraid of what might happen. Don't become a self-fulfilling prophecy."

I swallowed hard as my mom and Greer came back into the living room, stopping by the cheese platter. I let the subject drop, as we shifted to talk about the businesses and an upcoming holiday. Greer and Ford fit right in, as if they'd always been there, as if this was meant to be.

I saw the way they looked at each other, how Ford pulled Greer onto his lap, as she laughed and hopped right off him. Everyone joked, and this felt right.

But I knew I was holding back, and my dad did too.

It felt like sometimes I was waiting for my two friends to fall for each other and leave me behind. And I hated that. Because I wanted them. I wanted *this*.

But not everybody was as lucky as my parents. Not everybody was as lucky as my friends who seemed to find their forevers.

But I needed to live in the moment, to just breathe.

Because if I kept worrying, I would lose it all.

And I wasn't sure if I wanted to voice exactly what I craved.

But as Greer smiled at me, and Ford laughed with my family, I pushed those thoughts from my mind, and let myself be.

At least for now.

Chapter 17
GREER

THE SIRENS AND LIGHTS WENT OFF ABOVE THE GOAL AS the Avs scored, and I threw up my hands, screaming along with the guys on either side of me.

"Yes! Goal baby!" Ford cheered, and I shook my head, glaring at him. "You're supposed to be taking it easy."

"It's been a week. I'm fine. The Avs just scored!"

"It's about time," Noah grumbled, and I elbowed him in the side.

He grabbed me and kissed me hard.

I rolled my eyes, then went back to cheering with the others.

"I'm going to go get another beer, you want one?" Noah asked. Ford nodded and I shook my head.

"I'm fine with just water. Do you mind?"

"Of course not. Have fun."

He kissed me again, and I retook my seat, enjoying the boisterous crowd as the Avs went back on the ice.

"I think you're good luck."

"Am I?"

"Of course. You were good luck for the Rockies game too."

"I think we just have some kick ass teams."

"Damn straight we do," the man from behind me said, the woman on his arm nodding in agreement.

I turned to grin at them. "I really do think so."

"You know, I was really confused when you guys first sat down, because I thought you and the other dude were together," the woman said, her voice slightly slurred.

I stiffened for a moment, but I had to get used to this. I wasn't moving out of the guys' place anytime soon, and I didn't want to change anything. So that meant I was going to have to deal with the rest of the world when they saw us out together. I knew we were probably not even the only poly relationship in this stadium, but we were the only ones sitting in front of this woman. I really hoped that she wasn't going to react poorly.

"Oh. We're just here for the game."

"And it's a good one," Ford said, an easy smile on his

face, but I knew him well enough to see the tension at the corner of his eyes.

"Seriously though girl, these guys are hot together. But if you're with the other one, then you should totally give me his number," she said as she gestured towards Ford. "My friend just broke up with her boyfriend and is totally looking for a hot guy who likes hockey. What do you say?"

Out of the corner of my eye I saw her date wince, and then start whispering something to the man beside him, but I ignored it. Or at least I tried to.

Ford gave that easy smile again and shook his head. "I say go Avs. I'm taken though."

"Oh. Well, either way, you're hot, and I really thought that you were their sister or something." She smiled as she said it, but I saw the look in her eyes. She wanted to know the dirt, wanted to know details.

I wasn't in the mood to give it. I sat back and watched the game, my enthusiasm from earlier dimmed.

"You okay?"

"Of course I am. I'm watching my hockey team kick ass."

"Thank God, it took forever," Noah said as he handed over a beer to Ford, and then me a water. "I watched that last part standing up next to the lady at security."

"I'm sorry you missed it."

"I didn't miss anything. I've got you."

"Oh that's sweet," the lady mumbled behind us. Noah frowned. I shook my head in response.

"Come on, let's see what our boys do."

"Fuck yeah," Ford said, a little too much cheer in his tone.

I took a deep breath, then went back to watching the game, ignoring the woman whispering behind me, and I could see the guys she was with staring at us, trying to see what we were doing.

It didn't help that Ford had kissed me when we first sat down, and now had his hand on my knee. Noah put his arm around my shoulder, but wasn't even touching Ford. If anything, it looked like we were just three friends hanging out, only there was a vibe between us, there always was.

When the game ended and we made our way down the escalators, I fell back, watching the two of them laugh together. They gestured towards one another, speaking in hushed tones. They looked at each other like they knew. Like they had been waiting all this time for this moment.

"Whore," a woman mumbled beside us, and I realized she was the woman that had sat on the other side of the drunk woman behind us. And she was even drunker than the first woman.

I blinked, wondering if she was actually talking to me, before she sneered. "God is going to judge you." Then she flipped me off, tripped over her heels, and threw up in the trashcan.

People booed, and some clapped, and I moved away.

Ford was at my side then, Noah holding my hand. I felt cold and I just wanted to go home.

"Are you okay?"

"I'm fine. Let's just get back to the house."

I didn't want to say home. Because that was their home. And I was just staying there while I figured out my next steps. But I hadn't been figuring them out, I'd gotten used to this. Comfortable. And I should have remembered. I should have done better.

"Greer, talk to us."

I ignored Noah and gestured towards the door. "Come on, we're in the way. Let's just get out of here, okay? The Avs won. We should be happy."

They looked at each other as if they were having a silent conversation.

They were meant for each other. They got each other.

And I needed to remember the promise I had made when I first moved in.

So I put a smile on my face and followed them out to the car. I got in the backseat, needing a moment to breathe, to come to terms with what I needed to do.

Because this potential purgatory I had put myself in wasn't going to work.

I saw the way that others judged them, the way that they called me out for just being near them. And I could deal with that, I could deal with the hate, the judgment, but I couldn't deal with the pain that they would have to endure.

And in the end, they had always been meant for each other.

When we made it to the house, Ford took my hand and scowled.

"What did that woman say? What the hell happened? Was it about what the other lady said at the game?"

"What the hell did I miss?"

"This bitch behind us was making jokes and trying to figure out what our relationship was. She tried to get my number for a friend, assumed that the two of us were dating, and then the two of you. She just kept muttering on about random shit because she wanted the details."

"You don't need to call her a bitch. She was just saying what everyone else was thinking."

"What the hell?" Noah roared.

I blinked, wondering where this hostility came from. But then again, it had been a long couple weeks. A lot of things had happened, and we hadn't dealt with them. Maybe it was time to.

"I've really enjoyed being with you guys." Ford opened his mouth to say something but I held out my hand. "I've loved it. I have been so grateful to you guys for letting me stay here, to get my feet under me. And I'm ready. I can figure out the next steps, but I've needed this time. And we've had fun."

Noah snorted, and I nearly agreed with him. Because fun was such a small word for it. But I had let myself believe and I needed to do better. Because the two of them? They fit. Maybe they needed a moment of fun to push them into this. But I never wanted them to deal with the looks and the whispers. I was in the way. I was relying on them for everything, and not being the adult I needed to be.

I was in a holding pattern, and I was stopping them from living the next part of their lives. I had been living in this dream, and they deserved more than me being a third wheel.

I deserved more than that too.

"I think it's time for me to move in with Raven and Sebastian."

"You've got to be fucking kidding me?" Ford blurted. "After all this time? We fit. Don't you see that?"

"I know, it's been fun."

"If you say fun one more time I'm going to toss you over my lap and spank your ass," Noah blurted.

I shook my head. "I just, you heard what that lady said, you know you did, Ford. You were right there."

Ford shook his head. "You're not a whore."

Noah cursed again, and my lips twitched even though I was holding back tears. "I know I'm not. But other people are going to think that. And you guys are just so good for each other."

"We're good together, the three of us. Don't you realize that?"

I shook my head. "I don't know. I just, I don't want to feel like I'm standing in the way of you two being together."

"You're not standing in the way, you're standing beside us, between us. In the best fucking way possible," Noah shouted, and Ford nodded.

"Noah and I were fighting, trying to figure out what we could be together, but you want to know what the problem was? We were missing you."

I pressed my lips together. "No. You guys fit."

"With you," Ford countered.

"But I don't even know if this could work. I'm just so afraid that you guys are going to wake up and realize that you are best friends and lovers forever for a reason. And I'm an add-on and barnacle that won't let go."

"If you call yourself a fucking barnacle I will spank you for real," Noah added.

"Please stop saying spanking, it is not helping the situation," Ford said.

"Where the hell is this coming from? We were fine. We've been fine. What's going on?"

"It can't just be the hockey game and what those people said. Because we've been out as a threesome before. Maybe people look at us, or maybe they're just dealing with their own fucking lives. I am a kid who grew up with three parents. And yes it was weird sometimes, but it doesn't faze at least ninety percent of people. We live in a world where that doesn't fucking matter anymore. My parents helped make laws to ensure that their kids would be okay surviving in a world where poly relationships were legal. I know exactly what it feels like to live in a world where that's something that's normal. So that's not it. Talk to us."

I wiped away a tear, hating myself for breaking.

"I moved in because of the fire, for which we still don't have answers, and I'm not even looking for a place to live because of the insurance."

"So? We like you here." Ford moved forward.

I didn't move back, I should, but I let him hold my hand. "Ford—"

"No. You're wrong. You're not a barnacle, you're not just standing here. You're everything. So no, you don't get to do this. You don't get to run away."

"I'm not running away," I said quickly, hackles rising. "I just think you guys are perfect for each other."

"Yeah? We are. And you are perfect with us," Noah snapped.

Ford looked over at Noah. "Thank you for finally saying that, by the way, and I'm glad that we're having this conversation. Because I want to be with both of you. I like being with both of you. And no, it's not conventional, but fuck convention. What's it ever done for us anyway?"

"You guys."

"What?" Noah asked. "Are you going to let some drunk lady who threw random slurs at you and then threw up on herself judge you? Are you going to let that person tell you who you're allowed to be with? Because if so, we're going to have to sit down and actually talk this out."

"For a minute I thought you were going to threaten to spank her," Ford mumbled and I snorted out a laugh.

"This is serious." I said, rubbing my hands over my face.

"Of course it is. So let's talk it out, us three. Right now." Ford nodded.

Noah cleared his throat. "My dad said that the hardest part of their relationship, and the part that is the most important, is actually communicating. So this is what I want. I want both of you. I want things to remain as they are while we figure out how we are as the three of us. I don't want you to move out, I like you staying here. I like the fact that we work in the same building and we still have some time apart. I don't want you to go away."

"I thought you were going to walk away first," Ford said, and Noah took a step back, before he nodded.

"You know what, fair. Because I thought I would."

I put my hand over my chest, ignoring the hurt. It was selfish of me because I was the one that just tried to break up with them.

"I was going to walk away because I thought you two were perfect for each other. And I didn't want to be in the way." Then he looked me directly in the eyes. "But as I hear myself say the words, I realize how idiotic it is because I want you both, so I'm going to fucking fight for you. So, you need to fight for us too, Greer."

"I just don't want you to hate me if I'm standing in the way."

Ford cupped my face and crushed his mouth to mine.

"Never. I love you, Greer."

I froze, the words washing over me. I had hoped, had dreamed, but I never thought he would say them.

Noah cursed, and we both looked over at him.

"I should have added that to my statement," he said, waving his hand in the air. "I love you both. I have no idea what I'm doing here, I've never known what I'm doing—isn't that evident enough with Ford? I mean, I almost fucked up our friendship and relationship long before you even moved here, Greer. But I'm trying not to fuck it up now. I love you both. Now, please stay, don't leave, and let's figure out how to do this. It's going to be hard, but I fucking want it, so I'm going to fight for it. Finally."

Tears were freely falling from my cheeks as Noah pulled me away from Ford, and kissed me hard, before leaning over me to kiss him. I stood between them, my body shaking, as I tried to catch up with everything that had just happened.

"I thought I was going to leave tonight."

"Well, you can't. You're stuck with us." Noah looked at me expectantly.

It was then I realized I hadn't actually voiced my feelings out loud.

"I'm so fucking scared," I whispered. "But I love you both. I just really hope I don't mess this up."

"I stopped listening after you said I love you," Ford said with a laugh before he kissed me again, and then I leaned into them both and tried to breathe, tried to focus.

"I'm going to mess this up."

"No, you're not." Noah paused. "It's my turn to mess it up."

"Excuse me, no, you've both had your turns, clearly it's mine," Ford said, and I laughed, leaning into Noah as Ford tucked my hair behind my ear.

"Fuck what anyone says about us. They don't know us," Ford whispered.

"It wasn't what they said, it sort of just pushed me into the whole fearful thing about you two wanting each other more than me."

Noah cursed. "Then that's on us for not saying what we feel. I'm not very good at it even though my family is."

"My family never tells each other how they feel unless it's sarcasm. So here we are." Ford kissed me again.

This wasn't going to be easy.

Nothing worth having was.

I let myself believe. If only for the moment.

THE NEXT MORNING, sore and exhausted from them both, I left them in bed and headed to the coffee shop, since I had to be in to work on the next delivery. And I also wanted to tell Raven exactly what happened the night before. I hadn't texted her like I wanted to, so she had no idea that I had almost lost everything, and might have gained everything in one night.

I still couldn't quite believe it, and I was sure if I

blinked everything would change again, but I didn't let myself think too hard.

I made my way down the farm road on the other side of the neighborhood so I could hit the highway on the back end, avoiding heavy early morning traffic. The guys would meet me at the coffee shop later, and then we would discuss the next phase of our relationship, whatever that may be.

As I had never been in a serious relationship before, I had no idea what to expect.

I was smiling, bouncing my head to the music, when I heard tires squeal.

I screamed.

A car hit me from the side, turning me the opposite direction, as glass shattered, metal screeched, and my head slammed into the back of the seat. I hadn't been going fast, and the airbags didn't deploy. When I skidded to a stop, my breaths coming in pants, I looked around, wondering who had just hit me.

"Oh my God."

I reached around for my phone, but it had fallen underneath the seat.

I bent over, trying to reach it, and accidentally hit call because there was a notification from Noah on the screen.

That was fine, because they could help me out like

they had with the fire. I tried to reach for it again before someone tapped on the glass.

I let out a little scream, surprised, and then looked to see someone I hadn't thought I would ever see again.

"Matt?" I asked, my voice high with shock.

He grinned, then slammed the edge of something metal against the glass. I threw my hands over my face, trying to protect my eyes and skin from the glass shards.

And then Matt was reaching into the door, unlocking it.

"It's about time. We need to talk."

The door was jammed though, and he couldn't open it. He began to curse, leaning forward. I undid my seatbelt, and somehow through all the adrenaline, was able to crawl to the other side of the car.

Matt. It couldn't be my ex-boyfriend. It didn't make any sense. Had he hit me with the car? No. Matt, the sweet and unassuming guy who I barely even thought of anymore couldn't be coming after me with a knife, unless I had hit my head harder than I thought.

I practically rolled out of the passenger side of the car and looked around, hoping there was another vehicle around.

I hadn't been able to pick up my phone, but it was early enough in the morning that the streetlights were still on and there were no other cars on the road. Off in the distance I could hear the highway, but they wouldn't be able to hear me.

"I told you not to go. I told you that you were mine. And now, I'm going to make sure."

He began to walk around the front of the car, and I turned on my heels and ran off the side of the road, into the farmland. My heart racing, I prayed. I had to make it to a neighborhood, to help. Because something was wrong, and I did not think this was a dream.

Chapter 18
NOAH

FORD'S HAND SLID UP MY HIP AS I LEANED AGAINST THE counter, bringing the mug of coffee to my lips. I took a sip, and he grinned at me.

"You doing okay?" I asked, before taking another sip of coffee. I'd added enough sugar and cream to this to probably scare Greer, but I needed the extra kick. We hadn't slept much the night before, all of us celebrating one another.

It was nice, damn nice, but I was still getting the hang of things. And I wasn't quite awake.

"I'm doing just fine. Now though, I could probably use some of that coffee."

"Get your own. I'm very greedy this morning."

"You weren't that greedy when my cock was down your throat when we first woke up."

I held back a shiver, shaking my head at his antics. Greer had gone off to work, and the two of us had woken each other up slowly. With Greer's work hours, the three of us didn't always get up together, but we were going to figure it out. After all, this was it. What more did we need?

"Great, now I have a hard-on before we head to work." I pointedly looked down at my dick, and Ford laughed.

"I'm so sorry, darling. I would take care of that but we're going to be late. We have a shit ton to do today, and then I want to get home and plan a trip."

He moved away from me, and I missed him crowding me at the counter. He went to make himself a to-go mug of coffee as I drained mine, before going to make my own to-go cup. It really had been a long night, and we had not slept enough.

"A trip?"

"Yeah. I know we're all working, and we have the new client interviews since we need to fill the gaps from dropping the other ones." Ford scowled a bit at that, and I joined him.

We were no longer working with two clients who made our life a living hell, and between an upcoming event that Gus and Jennifer were going to be working on their own, and an event for Cage Enterprises, we were going to be busy. I honestly didn't know how a trip would fit into that.

"Maybe just a weekend, or something. I know that Greer works nearly every day because she loves her shop, but we need it. We're really good living here, the three of us. And now I want to do a bit more. To treat her. What do you think?"

"I think if we can make it work, it sounds amazing. But getting our three schedules to work? It's going to be hell."

"Getting three of our lives to blend together is going to be a good kind of hell, we'll figure it out." Ford leaned forward and pressed a kiss to my lips. I smiled against him, then groaned when the phone rang.

"I didn't know you had the ringer on."

"I left it on last night. But hey. It's our girl."

I smiled at Greer's name on the screen, as Ford answered on speakerphone.

"Hey babe. Did you forget something here?"

All we could hear were muffled sounds, maybe something moving. I frowned.

"Is her phone in her bag? Did she accidentally call us?"

But I straightened, alarm running through me. Something was wrong.

"Matt?" Greer's voice sounded higher than normal, fear in her tone.

"Matt?" I asked, and Ford shushed me.

Matt was her ex-boyfriend. Where the hell was she?

And then there was the sound of breaking glass and a scream. I grabbed my keys and bolted for the door.

"Her phone's on, I'm going to check the app to see where she is."

We had put all of us on the same security app when she had moved in, especially after the fire, so we knew where everyone was in case of an emergency. But I honest to God never thought we'd actually have to use it.

"It's about time. We need to talk."

Matt's voice was deep and dangerous, as if there was something wrong with it.

"Jesus Christ." I practically ran to the car, Ford on my heels.

"Track her."

"On it."

"I told you not to go. I told you that you were mine. And now, we're going to make sure."

And then the phone went dead. I looked at Ford and cursed.

"I don't know what happened. But damn it. What the hell is he doing?"

"If he's hurt her, I'll kill him," I growled, as I pulled up her phone on the app.

"The call must have ended, though I don't know

how." I shook my head. "But it's still on. And it's only a couple of miles away."

"I'm calling the team, and the authorities."

"Do it, I'll get us there."

"She has to be okay."

"Damn straight," I growled, and then everything clicked.

"Fuck," I growled as Ford looked over at me as I sped out of the neighborhood.

"What?"

"All those little attacks? The fire? The broken things at work and the lost documents and the cashews and everything. Someone was fucking with her all this time and we knew it, but we couldn't piece it together."

I looked over at Ford before I turned the corner, and the anger on his face seared me.

"The primroses."

I slammed my hand on the steering wheel so hard it nearly broke. "And we fucking missed it." *I* missed it again. I kept missing things, things I should have seen, things it was my fucking job to see. And now people I loved were going to be hurt because of it. I wasn't going to let this happen again. Never fucking again.

"She hates primroses, and he would've known that. He sent them to her how many times?" I asked.

"I don't know. I think twice, maybe more. It kept

slipping to the side because of everything else. Jesus Christ."

I looked forward again at Ford's exclamation and slammed on the brakes when I came to the site of an accident.

There was already a car pulled over to the side, an older gentleman looking around with his phone to his ear.

"I don't know what happened. I don't know where the drivers are. But they're not here."

A good Samaritan, then.

"There're footprints over here," Ford said as we ran towards the car.

Someone had slammed their car into her, just enough to make her stop, but hopefully not enough to hurt her. But how was I supposed to fucking know?

"Looks like she ran this way."

"Sirs? What's going on?" the good Samaritan said.

"I already called the authorities," Ford said to the other man. "Let them know that we're going after her. The guy who hit her with his car is chasing her."

The man's eyes widened. "How could you know that?"

"Because she's ours," I said, even though it probably didn't make any sense to him. We moved through the field, and I hoped Greer was going towards the neighborhood. The field was a watershed farm that was between the two different neighborhoods. It was on the back end of the highway, and probably wouldn't be developed for a long time because it was in a flood zone when the snow melted fast. It was good for the farmers who knew what they were doing, but not great right now since the field was muddy and hard to move in.

"You should have stayed back. You just got out of the hospital."

Ford glared at me. "I got out of the hospital last week. And you don't get to leave me behind when our woman is hurt and scared."

Our woman, damn it. Fuck yes.

"She's ours, we're not going to let this guy hurt her again."

"Damn straight. Let's go."

We followed her footprints as quickly as we could. From the skids and long trails, it looked as if she fell a couple of times, but got up and kept moving. If she was hurt, if there was a fucking scratch on her, I was going to rip that man's head from his shoulders.

"So, he was stalking her this whole time? Fucking with her?" Ford asked, his voice low in case we were overheard.

"Sounds like. And I missed it."

Ford glared at me. "No. Don't do this. We're going to have a talk."

I didn't need a talk, I needed to find her.

There was a scream, and we started running as fast as we could. And then without saying anything, Ford gestured that he would circle around, and I nodded, knowing it was better if we came at him from two sides, to get a better handle on the situation.

Our team and the cops were on their way, but they would be too late. We had to help her.

Ford moved around, ducking behind a large reed or whatever the hell this farm was growing.

"Matt. Put down the knife. You don't have to do this. We can talk. I promise."

Anger roiled in my gut. The man had a knife? Jesus Christ.

"You were supposed to be mine. We were supposed to be forever. You never saw that. You never cared. You just went about your business like I didn't matter. I tried to show you that I cared, tried to take you out of that place that you hated. You could have lived with me, in a home that I own, not rent like a poor person."

"Matt, please. You don't have to do this."

"Fuck you. I burned down that place so you could live with me, instead you went to them like a whore."

I slid through the clearing, my gaze narrowed as I watched a man with blondish hair, broad shoulders, and a manic expression on his face, move closer to Greer. She had her muddy hands up, a few cuts and scrapes on her face, and just the sight of her blood made me want to reach out and kill the bastard.

I needed to stop him.

Out of the corner of my eye I saw Ford come closer, and he nodded at me.

We could do this, disarm him. As long as he only had the knife. When Ford moved closer, I knew he would distract him, and I would have to stop him.

For the people that I loved? I'd do anything.

I just had to be enough this time.

"Greer? Are you okay?" Ford asked as he came from the side, and Matt whirled towards him, knife waving in the air.

"You? How the hell are you here? You took her from me, you asshole."

"We can talk about that, Matt. Why don't you put the knife down? You don't need to hurt anyone."

"Fuck you. She was mine. She isn't perfect, but I was going to make her perfect. My parents would've loved her. I wanted her to love me the way that she should have. I took away everything that was too much for her so she wouldn't have to worry. I took away her house, and part of her work. Then you were in the way. *You*. And you couldn't even die when I needed you to."

I moved silently, holding back the curse I wanted to scream at him. So, it was Matt who had somehow gotten cashews into the fucking building. I could not believe this guy had done all of that, and we hadn't known. Then again, we hadn't been looking for him. Hadn't realized anyone was after her.

We had been so damn wrong.

"Matt, you don't have to do this. We can just talk."

"I'm done talking. I'm done waiting. You're going to be mine, and this asshole is going to be gone."

He moved forward, slicing out. It wasn't Ford he went after, but Greer. I moved as quickly as I could as Ford jumped between Matt and Greer, holding up his arm in defense.

Ford didn't even make a sound when the knife sliced his arm, he just glared and pushed Matt back.

Greer tried to get around Ford, probably to see what she could do to help stanch the blood.

I moved stealthily, coming up behind Matt. That fucker didn't even see me as I reached around him, gripped his wrist, and twisted. The weasel let out a scream of pain as I snapped his wrists, the knife falling to the ground. I pushed the guy down, a knee at his back, and looked over at Ford and Greer.

"You two okay?"

"It's just a shallow slice. Asshole. I didn't know what he was going to do with it, I just needed to make sure he didn't hit Greer."

"You could have died. He wasn't going to hurt me. He was just threatening me."

Greer took off her light jacket and wrapped it around Ford's arm. "I can't believe you guys found me."

"You made a trail, and you called us. We'll always find you," I said, as I looked up at the two of them.

Matt writhed beneath me, crying in pain—I had broken his wrists, but I didn't care.

I heard stomping through the grass, and I tried to figure out what the hell we were going to do if he had backup, and then Daisy was there, pajama bottoms on, hair in a messy bun, and gun in hand.

We were all licensed to carry, but we hadn't used our guns, hadn't needed to.

When she saw us, she sighed and shook her head. "Well, that's one way to wake up."

"Cops are on their way," Gus said as he slid through the forested part of the farmland. "Told them that we were on site too, and we're licensed to carry. Just so you're aware."

Daisy shrugged. "Was he working with anyone else?"

I pressed my knee down into Matt's back. "Were you?"

"No," he whined. "I just wanted Greer."

"You never had me," Greer said, her voice strong, though I saw tears in her eyes. I couldn't move yet, so Ford held her as the authorities came forward.

Daisy started to explain things, showed her license, and I got up, letting the authorities take care of Matt. I moved forward and put my arms around Ford and Greer.

Greer broke down then, Ford cursed, and I just held them, knowing that I'd almost lost them today.

"We need to get you guys checked out. We don't know what else you might have hurt, Greer."

"I'm fine, I promise."

"You're going to see a doctor," Ford snapped.

"Then so are you. You need stitches."

I nearly fell to my knees, because it was over. The authorities were taking care of Matt, and as the EMTs came forward, I gestured so they could look at the two people I loved the most.

"I love you," I whispered to both of them as we separated and the EMTs started to look them each over.

I glared at the man who had caused all of this. He seemed so unassuming. Just looked like a nice guy who had never done anything.

But in the end that man didn't matter.

Ford and Greer did. And they would be okay. We would all be okay.

But damn, I was never letting them out of my sight again.

I loved them, and I was never letting go.

Chapter 19
GREER

"I'M FINE, REALLY, YOU DON'T NEED TO KEEP TUCKING ME in on the couch."

I looked up at Ford, who had a scowl on his face.

"You know there's no stopping him right now, right?" I said.

Ford sighed. "I guess if I'm going to be pampered, it might as well be by you two."

"You two can pamper each other after I feed you. Just relax."

I raised a brow at Ford, who just sighed before I spoke. "You should sit with us and cuddle. We want to cuddle."

"As soon as I get this quiche out of the oven." He sounded so disgruntled that both Ford and I burst out laughing.

"You know damn well that I didn't cook this. My mom did. I hope that it doesn't have eggshells in it." Noah paused. "And if you tell my mother I said that, I will spank both your asses."

"That's really not a deterrent," I said, laughter still evident in my voice.

Ford grinned from beside me. "You know, we could see how much trouble we can get into on the couch."

"I swear to God if you guys start giving each other orgasms on that couch when I'm trying to make sure you are resting, I will spank your asses but not let either one of you come."

I shut my mouth then, eyes wide, and Ford just shook his head. "We really can't take him anywhere."

"Okay, I think we need to let it cool for a second, and then I'll serve it." Noah kept mumbling to himself, and I couldn't help but sigh as I looked at his back. He was trying so hard, and I knew he'd been damn scared. We all had.

But Noah was now becoming Mr. Domestic, something he was not very good at but at least was being cute about.

"I'm willing to bet that it is probably burned on the outside and cold on the inside," Ford mumbled, and I put my hand over my mouth, trying not to laugh.

"We're still going to eat it though, right?" I whispered, even though Noah was coming forward, and I knew he could hear us.

"Of course we are. Our man is cooking for us."

"You guys are ridiculous. There are enough casseroles and other things to heat up in that fridge and freezer to last us a lifetime. If you don't like the quiche, you can suck on it."

"You're really just asking for it, aren't you?" I asked, as Ford burst out laughing.

Noah pinched the bridge of his nose. "I'm still not okay with the whole being held at knife point and car accident thing. All because we didn't realize that Matt was a psychopath."

The humor immediately drained out of me, and I set my feet on the floor, ready to get up. But when Noah growled at me, I reached out and gripped his hand.

"It was not your fault. Nothing about this was your fault. You're not supposed to do background checks and psychological tests on every single person you meet. That is not your job."

"And yet some psychopath decided that if he couldn't have you, no one could. How are we supposed to deal with that?"

"By using a punching bag, by being with each other, knowing that Matt will never have her? How about forgiving yourself even though there's nothing to forgive."

With my free hand I reached out and gripped Ford's, my love for him overpowering everything except for my love for Noah. I didn't know how I got this lucky, to find this passion and this happiness with not one but two men.

I had never asked for this, had never thought it a possibility.

In fact, I distinctly remembered the day that I had been standing at my counter and watched the two of them walk by, smiles on their faces only for each other.

And in that instant, I had told myself I would never have them, so I walked away and tried to find happiness elsewhere.

That had been a mistake of epic proportions, but now I knew better. Now I had them.

"Matt doesn't matter. I don't know what else he will be charged with other than arson and attempted murder, and we'll deal with it, but he's going to be out of the picture. And now it's the three of us, and we're going to figure out this whole domesticity thing."

"Just like that, you're not even going to think about him?" Noah asked, confusion etched on his face.

I leaned forward and cupped his cheek. "Yes. Because he's not worth it. The fact that I hadn't even really thought of him since we broke up tells you that. There's something wrong with Matt, but that's on him.

Not on us. And now that the insurance and my former landlords are getting what they want, I can move on."

"You're not moving out, are you?" Ford blurted.

I shook my head, holding back a laugh. "I really wasn't expecting to live with the two men that I love right away, but we did things backwards. And that's fine. We're going to have to have some ground rules and communication, but no, I'm not planning on moving out."

"I would say we're not going to let you move out, but that borders on the whole growly possessive thing."

"It's hot when you two do it because I realize that even though you are growly and possessive, you'll also not force me to do anything I don't want to do. It's a weird dynamic where trust is involved. Imagine that."

Ford shook his head. "So, are you going to keep your own room? Or are we going to make it a guest room again?"

I bit my lip and drew circles with my fingers on the blanket. "I like the fact that we all have separate rooms right now." Horatio jumped on my lap, following my finger, and I slid my fingers through his fur, amazed that he was letting me pet him. Of course, as soon as I thought that, he jumped onto Ford's lap. Ford gave me an apologetic look.

Well, at least I had the love of two men, I suppose I'd

have to work on Horatio. He might love me, but he was still a little too skittish.

"I like being able to have our space, but also being able to sleep in each other's rooms. Maybe that'll change one day, maybe we'll find something different. But I like being able to wake up every morning next to you two, but also know that if you two need to wake up together, or if it's our turn for date night, we have that option."

"You say that, but you know you're just going to be sleeping between us most nights," Ford said slyly.

I laughed, I couldn't help it. "True. But the meager possessions I own are in that room, and I like having my own space since Matt took it from me."

Noah nodded tightly, gripping my hand. "Okay, so we keep our separate spaces, but I'm never going to not want you next to me. I love you, Greer."

I blushed, still in awe that these men loved me.

"I love you both. And yes, I'm excited about what's to come, and I know there's a thousand things we need to do, to plan, just to live at this point, but I am not going anywhere."

"That's all I really needed you to say." Ford winced as his phone buzzed, and then he looked up at me.

"Okay, I should just warn you, we've held them back as long as we could."

I looked between my men, and then down at Horatio. "What's happening?"

"The families have arrived. They gave us three days. There's no stopping them."

The doorbell rang and Noah went to open it, and Montgomerys, Cages, and even Cassidys walked through the door.

My eyes filled as my brothers came forward, and plucked me off the couch to hold me tight.

Noah tried to warn them off me, saying I was too sore from the accident, but I waved him away.

"That's it, we're wrapping you in bubble wrap," Heath growled.

"Oh, we can do that. We have tons of bubble wrap," Noah's mom replied.

Ford's eldest brother was looking down at his arm, scowling. "And you're sure it's fine? You don't need to change the bandage or anything?"

"I'm fine. I'm following doctor's orders. I swear. Though I can't believe you all arranged to be here at once."

"There may be a group chat involved," Aston said primly.

I met my brothers' gazes, and they looked just as overwhelmed as I did.

I wasn't used to family, not with the way my parents had raised us, but I was getting a chance now. With my brothers, and with my two men and their families.

"I guess small holidays and family dinners are a thing

of the past aren't they?" I asked, completely overwhelmed as the Montgomerys took my brothers in.

"Oh honey, you have no idea," Noah's mom said as
she kissed my temple.

I found myself on the couch again, settled between
my men as everybody moved around and helped themselves to food, ignoring the eggshells in the quiche.

I had fallen for best friends, had been tempted into
the most scorching of dreams.

But as Horatio jumped into my lap again, and began
to purr, I breathed a sigh of relief.

We were going to make this work. Jobs and families
and decisions and homes. We would find a way to live in
a future where I would never be alone again.

I had my brothers, big families, and the loves of my
life.

I didn't need anything else.

Just them.

Chapter 20
DAISY

"I'LL BE SAFE, BIG BROTHER." I ROLLED MY EYES AS I spoke into the phone, making my way down the street.

"I'm not your brother, I'm your cousin."

"More like second cousin fifteen times removed."

I could hear the roll of Noah's eyes as he responded, but it was our own little joke. We Montgomerys liked to make things complicated. It also didn't help that technically I wasn't even related by blood to the Montgomerys. I was adopted by my mother, Adrian, who was a Montgomery. My father had always been there for me, no matter what, and had let the Montgomerys assimilate me, even though he and his family were just as strong, just as loud and exuberant. I had two sets of loving families, and I was grateful for it. But that also meant they were overbearing, and never quite let me do things on my own. It didn't matter that I was older than Noah, that I was in fact the oldest member of the security team. I had founded the place with Noah and Ford, but because they were men, the rest of the world assumed that they were the sole owners. And if it wasn't them, it was my other cousins, Kane and Kingston. I was usually thought of as the secretary. No, my cousins and everyone else who worked with us never assumed that. They never put me in that role. If anyone was the person in charge of paperwork at Montgomery Security, it was Noah. But it didn't help that when men with big pockets and bigger egos came in, they assumed I was the little lady who should be in a pencil skirt and tights.

But that wasn't my job. Today, I was checking out a new warehouse for security purposes.

"Is Kingston on his way?" I asked, knowing that Noah would know. Noah always knew.

"He should be. He's caught in traffic on 25."

"Shocking. Traffic on 25. You're going to need to alert the media. Whatever shall they do with this brand-new information."

"You would think with every lane that they add, it would get better, but somehow it doesn't. It's like they narrow the lanes or something. I just don't understand it."

"This is why we're not civil engineers, big brother."

"Again, not your brother. You're the old one. Remember?"

"Older. Not old. I'm about to go have your boyfriend or your girlfriend beat the crap out of you."

"Because I have a boyfriend and a girlfriend. Look at me, so fancy."

That made me smile. The fact that Noah was now laughing and joking and not so growly meant that perhaps Greer and Ford were finally bringing him out of his shell. It was good to see.

Even if I wasn't used to it.

"Well, have Kingston meet me. I'm going to check out the warehouse, see how security is set up. Our client's going to want us having top-notch security here, as well as both a male and a female bodyguard."

"That's why you and Kingston are on it. Are you going to wait for him?"

"There's no need, I won't go past the front area."

"Okay, keep me posted."

"Always do."

I ended the call but made sure that my locator was turned on. It was just a little thing on the phone, to make sure that they always knew where we were. It was another layer of security.

I was the most suited of us to being a bodyguard, though it didn't seem like it. I was smaller, more slender, and only one of two women in the department.

CARRIE ANN RYAN

Jennifer was taller than me, a little more muscular, and damn good at casing out security. And I was glad we hired her and Gus over the past few months. Not only was it nice to have some more estrogen in the house, it was nice to have their skills. But it was me on the case today, and because I had the most experience, I would be leading the team on this one. Despite what the clients wanted.

They didn't want a little lady protecting them, but the client's wife wanted me, and therefore I would do what I could.

We were on the far east side of Denver, in a not so nice neighborhood, but it was up and coming. In other words, the city was using higher property taxes from new neighborhoods to clear out what they didn't want and to put in what they did. I wasn't sure how I felt about that exactly, but if it meant actually using some of the land wisely instead of polluting it, I was up for that. Some of my family members were in the construction business, and while they didn't tend to work on projects like this, they might at some point.

My phone buzzed again and my other cousin's name popped up on text. Aria had worked in security with us, but now worked with another subsidiary, one that fit her skills better. I missed her working with us day in and day out, but it made sense. Too many Montgomerys in one room tended to make people a little unnerved. Plus, Aria was younger than all of us and was still finding her way. I was just grateful that we were able to give her that.

Aria: *Girls' trip next month?*

I frowned and thought back to my calendar before texting back.

Me: *I think so. I'll check my calendar when I get off site. But yes, girls' trip sounds fun.*

Aria: *Be safe. I'll plan it. Love you.*

I smiled.

Me: *Love you too, and I know you'll plan it.*

I slid my phone back into my pocket, and got back on the job. Kingston should be there any minute, but I wanted to get the lay of the land. It was just an empty warehouse, no sounds, but the clients had purchased the property recently and wanted to make sure that it was secure.

I wasn't sure what for yet, that was Noah's job, but once I was through with the research, I'd know the ins and outs of every single thing they were doing.

I loved my job. Truly.

I just wondered exactly what came next. I had my job, my family, and the girls' trip coming, but that was it. No other plans, no dates set up, no big friend groups outside of my family. I had fallen into this, much like I had fallen into a few other things, and I guess it made sense. With such a big family, with the way we blended together, it was harder to make outside friendships like

Noah had with Ford. Then again, the two were now together along with Greer, so maybe it wasn't so complicated.

Maybe I just needed to find someone for me.

Or maybe I needed to get my mind on the task and do what I was good at.

Work.

Because that was all I did.

I frowned as I looked at the shabby structure, and assumed the place was just going to be torn down anyway. I didn't know why they needed us in here, but I would come in and I would work.

I looked around, but froze at the sound of a click.

It didn't sound like a gun cocking, but more likc metal against metal.

It didn't make any sense. The sound of a car coming closer echoed throughout the warehouses, and I turned to see Kingston's truck moving forward. Relief slid into me, and I hadn't realized how tense I was until I relaxed at the sight. I turned to wave at him as I heard another click, and my adrenaline surged. Kingston's tires squealed as he slammed on the brakes, but there was nothing he could do.

The explosion hit hard and fast, and all I could do was throw my hands over my face to protect myself from the flames, and as I hit the ground, I heard Kingston screaming, running toward me, but then there was nothing.

Just darkness.

And a promise never kept.

IF YOU'D LIKE TO READ A BONUS SCENE FROM GREER,
NOAH & FORD:
CHECK OUT THIS SPECIAL EPILOGUE!

NEXT IN THE SERIES:
Daisy and Hugh change everything in Last First Kiss

A Note from Carrie Ann Ryan

Thank you so much for reading **BEST FRIEND TEMPTATION!**

When I plotted this book, I wanted it to break my heart and be scorching so I hope that worked! These three made me so happy and I knew their book would be a stepping stone in the series.

Now...what's next? Things are about to get...explosive.

Daisy meets her match with Hugh (a new hero) in Last First Kiss. This book is...just wait. Because I'm fanning myself as I write it.

And those brothers you met? Yep...they are ALL getting books.

Greer's brothers get their own series called the First Time series. Heath will be book 1 in Good Time

Boyfriend!! Three brothers. Three books. And all the emotional heat. Because the Cassidy brothers are moving to Denver and everything is about to change.

And as for Ford's brothers? Well….it won't be a secret for you because The Cage Brothers will begin soon. Make sure you're signed up for my newsletter so you know when you can hear more because keeping this series secret is SO HARD!

The Montgomery Ink Legacy Series:
   Book 1: Bittersweet Promises
   Book 2: At First Meet
   Book 2.5: Happily Ever Never
   Book 3: Longtime Crush
   Book 4: Best Friend Temptation
   Book 5: Last First Kiss

IF YOU'D LIKE TO READ A BONUS SCENE FROM GREER,
NOAH & FORD:
CHECK OUT THIS SPECIAL EPILOGUE!

NEXT IN THE SERIES:
Daisy and Hugh change everything in Last First Kiss

If you want to make sure you know what's coming next from me, you can sign up for my newsletter at www.

CarrieAnnRyan.com; follow me on twitter at @CarrieAnnRyan, or like my Facebook page. I also have a Facebook Fan Club where we have trivia, chats, and other goodies. You guys are the reason I get to do what I do and I thank you.

Make sure you're signed up for my MAILING LIST so you can know when the next releases are available as well as find giveaways and FREE READS.

Happy Reading!

Also from Carrie Ann Ryan

The Montgomery Ink Legacy Series:

Book 1: Bittersweet Promises

Book 2: At First Meet

Book 2.5: Happily Ever Never

Book 3: Longtime Crush

Book 4: Best Friend Temptation

Book 5: Last First Kiss

The Wilder Brothers Series:

Book 1: One Way Back to Me

Book 2: Always the One for Me

Book 3: The Path to You

Book 4: Coming Home for Us

Book 5: Stay Here With Me

Book 6: Finding the Road to Us

Book 7: A Wilder Wedding

The First Time Series:
Book 1: Good Time Boyfriend
Book 2: Last Minute Fiance

The Aspen Pack Series:
Book 1: Etched in Honor
Book 2: Hunted in Darkness
Book 3: Mated in Chaos
Book 4: Harbored in Silence
Book 5: Marked in Flames

The Montgomery Ink: Fort Collins Series:
Book 1: Inked Persuasion
Book 2: Inked Obsession
Book 3: Inked Devotion
Book 3.5: Nothing But Ink
Book 4: Inked Craving
Book 5: Inked Temptation

The Montgomery Ink: Boulder Series:
Book 1: Wrapped in Ink
Book 2: Sated in Ink
Book 3: Embraced in Ink
Book 3: Moments in Ink
Book 4: Seduced in Ink

Also from Carrie Ann Ryan

Book 7.5: <u>Executive Ink</u>
Book 8: <u>Inked Memories</u>
Book 8.5: <u>Inked Nights</u>
Book 8.7: <u>Second Chance Ink</u>
Book 8.5: Montgomery Midnight Kisses
Bonus: Inked Kingdom

The On My Own Series:

Book 0.5: My First Glance
Book 1: My One Night
Book 2: My Rebound
Book 3: My Next Play
Book 4: My Bad Decisions

The Promise Me Series:

Book 1: Forever Only Once
Book 2: From That Moment
Book 3: Far From Destined
Book 4: From Our First

The Less Than Series:

Book 1: Breathless With Her
Book 2: Reckless With You
Book 3: Shameless With Him

The Fractured Connections Series:

Book 1: Breaking Without You

Book 2: Shouldn't Have You
Book 3: Falling With You
Book 4: Taken With You

The Whiskey and Lies Series:
Book 1: <u>Whiskey Secrets</u>
Book 2: <u>Whiskey Reveals</u>
Book 3: <u>Whiskey Undone</u>

The Gallagher Brothers Series:
Book 1: <u>Love Restored</u>
Book 2: <u>Passion Restored</u>
Book 3: <u>Hope Restored</u>

The Ravenwood Coven Series:
Book 1: Dawn Unearthed
Book 2: Dusk Unveiled
Book 3: Evernight Unleashed

The Talon Pack:
Book 1: <u>Tattered Loyalties</u>
Book 2: <u>An Alpha's Choice</u>
Book 3: <u>Mated in Mist</u>
Book 4: <u>Wolf Betrayed</u>
Book 5: <u>Fractured Silence</u>
Book 6: <u>Destiny Disgraced</u>
Book 7: <u>Eternal Mourning</u>

Book 8: <u>Strength Enduring</u>

Book 9: <u>Forever Broken</u>

Book 10: Mated in Darkness

Book 11: Fated in Winter

Redwood Pack Series:

Book 1: <u>An Alpha's Path</u>

Book 2: <u>A Taste for a Mate</u>

Book 3: <u>Trinity Bound</u>

Book 3.5: <u>A Night Away</u>

Book 4: <u>Enforcer's Redemption</u>

Book 4.5: <u>Blurred Expectations</u>

Book 4.7: <u>Forgiveness</u>

Book 5: <u>Shattered Emotions</u>

Book 6: <u>Hidden Destiny</u>

Book 6.5: <u>A Beta's Haven</u>

Book 7: <u>Fighting Fate</u>

Book 7.5: <u>Loving the Omega</u>

Book 7.7: <u>The Hunted Heart</u>

Book 8: <u>Wicked Wolf</u>

The Elements of Five Series:

Book 1: From Breath and Ruin

Book 2: From Flame and Ash

Book 3: From Spirit and Binding

Book 4: From Shadow and Silence

Dante's Circle Series:

Book 1: <u>Dust of My Wings</u>

Book 2: <u>Her Warriors' Three Wishes</u>

Book 3: <u>An Unlucky Moon</u>

Book 3.5: <u>His Choice</u>

Book 4: <u>Tangled Innocence</u>

Book 5: <u>Fierce Enchantment</u>

Book 6: <u>An Immortal's Song</u>

Book 7: <u>Prowled Darkness</u>

Book 8: Dante's Circle Reborn

Holiday, Montana Series:

Book 1: <u>Charmed Spirits</u>

Book 2: <u>Santa's Executive</u>

Book 3: <u>Finding Abigail</u>

Book 4: <u>Her Lucky Love</u>

Book 5: Dreams of Ivory

The Branded Pack Series:
(Written with Alexandra Ivy)

Book 1: <u>Stolen and Forgiven</u>

Book 2: <u>Abandoned and Unseen</u>

Book 3: <u>Buried and Shadowed</u>

About the Author

Carrie Ann Ryan is the New York Times and USA Today bestselling author of contemporary, paranormal, and young adult romance. Her works include the Montgomery Ink, Redwood Pack, Fractured Connections, and Elements of Five series, which have sold over 3.0 million books worldwide. She started writing while in graduate school for her advanced degree in chemistry and hasn't stopped since. Carrie Ann has written over seventy-five novels and novellas with more in the works. When she's not losing herself in her emotional and action-packed worlds, she's reading as much as she can while wrangling her clowder of cats who have more followers than she does.

www.CarrieAnnRyan.com